Wanted: Cat mum to corral two curious cats tangled up in murderous

A smart woman would dump her cheating ex, move from the city, and give herself a chance for a well-deserved do-over. A smarter woman—smarter than me, anyway—wouldn't jump out of that same frying pan and return to Cape Discovery, a seaside village where her family is the nuttiest of all the nut-ball residents.

I'm a high school counsellor turned new owner of Unraveled, my granddad's yarn store in town. More exciting than a delivery of rainbow colored wool is the news of movie location scouts in the area, though not everyone believes all publicity is good publicity. Game on between landowners to secure such a lucrative deal.

I can't help being caught up in movie fever, until I stumble onto one of those landowners, face down in a kitty litter tray. Deader than dead thanks to an unknown assailant. With dating disasters aplenty both online and in-real-life and a hitman on the loose, things couldn't get much more murderously crazy in Cape Discovery. If only that were true...

Tessa Wakefield has her hands full juggling a cozy craft store, her crazy family, and two men who'd rather poke out their eyes than describe themselves as cute. Which they totally are. Cute, charismatic, and occasionally on her mind when she's not stumbling over dead bodies and using her newfound sleuthing skills to track down murderers. Lucky she's an excellent multi-tasker because digging beneath Cape Discovery's surface can unearth secrets that kill.

HANKS AND A HITMAN

A KNITTY KITTIES MYSTERY

TRACEY DREW

ICON
PUBLISHING

Copyright © 2021 by Tracey Drew

All rights reserved.

No part of this book may be reproduced in any form or by any electronic or mechanical means, including information storage and retrieval systems, without written permission from the author, except for the use of brief quotations in a book review.

ISBN (Mobi): 978-0-473-54047-0

ISBN (Epub): 978-0-473-54046-3

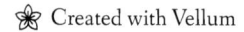

❦ Created with Vellum

ALSO BY TRACEY DREW

Knitty Kitties Mysteries

Knitted and Knifed
Purled and Poisoned
Hanks and a Hitman

FREE BOOK!

Want to read the prequel of Kit and Pearl's first crime-solving adventure? Click here to sign up to my newsletter and I'll send you a FREE e-copy of Balls & Bones!

ONE

IF THERE's one thing I'm better at than sniffing out clues and murderers, it's sniffing out chocolate. More precisely, chocolate Easter eggs at my family's annual camping trip and Easter egg hunt. You think my seven-year-old niece is competitive? She's got nothing on her thirty-five-year-old aunt: the 'Sexy Sleuth Saves the Day' extraordinaire.

Not my words, of course, but the name of a cocktail invented in my honor by a local, not so bad himself, bartender after I solved my last—*ahem*—homicide case.

In case you're one of the few unfamiliar with my notoriety, let me introduce myself. Tessa Wakefield's my name. Owning a yarn store in the deceptively quaint-looking seaside town of Cape Discovery is my game. Not quite as catchy as, say, catching killers is my game—but I suspect handing out business cards with that slogan might be inadvisable. I'm already on a certain police detective's watch list.

But the truth is, when this former high school guidance counselor isn't wrangling her family or two pesky cats, she has an unfortunate habit of stumbling over the recently deceased. And no, I don't moonlight as a morgue assistant.

It's not my fault if I'm proving, one body at a time, that I have a nose for murder.

Still, there's only so much excitement a girl can take before she requires some R&R. Though in this instance—a family Easter camping trip—there's not as much resting-and-recreationing as there is a raucous, rambunctious, ruthless dedication to drive the more senior Wakefields up the wall. With a New Zealand autumn in full swing, it might seem an odd time to take a family camping vacation. But that's my family in a nutshell.

Odd. But odd in a—mostly—nice way.

Except when it comes to finding foil-wrapped delights hidden beneath shrubs or tucked behind tent pegs.

Then all bets are off.

To ensure the *Great War of the Creme Eggs* and accusations of nepotism that occurred this time last year didn't erupt again, Granddad Harry had paid a couple of teenagers to hide the eggs while we prepared breakfast in the communal kitchen. Harry's our family's patriarch, and everyone, including my dad, refers to him by his first name. A retired cop, he's still formidable at eighty-mumble, despite our beloved Nana Dee-Dee having done her best to keep his ego in check.

Craftily, my two older sisters and their spouses volunteered for cleanup duties while our younger brother, Sean, and I, along with our parents and Harry, watched the kids run wild through the campground in search of a sugar rush.

While Harry—who'd traded in his usual knitted beanie for a floppy sunhat—stood at attention and hollered suggestions to his great-grandchildren, the rest of us positioned our camping chairs in the shade overlooking the wide swath of sandy beach. Yeah, we live by the ocean and go camping by it too. Go figure. We Wakefields have this 'odd' thing down pat.

Of course, New Zealand's Hawke's Bay has some of the country's most stunning and pristine beaches, so it's small wonder we can't get enough of them. Golden sand, wall-to-wall sunshine sparkling on cerulean waters, and birdsong from the abundance of native bush surrounding the campsite the only disturbance. A peaceful haven—or at least, it would be but for, you know...family.

"I had the most interesting conversation with Jessica the other day," Mum said, referring to a fellow real estate agent.

Sean stretched out his long legs and dedicated himself to the task of unwrapping a chocolate egg he'd pilfered from one of the kids. "Let me guess. Your multi-talented co-worker's offering another of her watercolors to the mid-winter gala for auction?"

Mum chuckled and swatted his arm. If I'd uttered even the tiniest hint of snark regarding Jessica's talent with a paintbrush, I'd have earned a maternal *behave yourself* glare. But Sean, the baby of our family, could do no wrong in his mummy's eyes.

"No, silly. She heard through the grapevine that location scouts for Pavlova Productions are poking around Cape Discovery properties this long weekend."

Pavlova Productions? While not quite in the same league as New Zealand's biggest claim to fame—Peter Jackson's WingNut Films—Pavlova was rapidly gaining ground in the booming national film industry. There were even online rumors that they'd scored a lucrative deal for a movie trilogy based on a series of books by an acclaimed Kiwi writer.

"Didn't those guys make the Hobbit movies?" Sean

licked chocolate off his fingers with more interest than his voice contained.

"No, that's Peter Jackson. Pavlova Productions did that dreadful horror movie where aliens that look like overweight octopi turn commuters into zombies. This time, they're doing a small town overrun by zombies."

Sean brightened. "Did she say whether they're gonna make the movie in town? Maybe they'll hold auditions for extras. I could totally do a zombie stagger." He leaped out of his seat and proceeded to demonstrate.

Mum smiled indulgently at my brother. "I'm sure if they hold an audition for zombies, you'll nail it, sweetie." She angled her head and winked at me as Sean grew bored of pitching about and wandered off in search of more Easter eggs.

I grinned back at her. "Did Jessica mention which properties they're looking at?"

"Wilsons' dairy farm, the MacKenzies', and Marcus Hall's."

"The MacKenzies? As in, Bridget MacKenzie?" Bridget MacKenzie, or Birdie as most knew her by, ran an animal rescue charity from her ten-acre block of land. She also owned Birdie's Clowder Motel, where cats were spoiled rotten in the way they felt they deserved while their owners were away on vacation. "Birdie wouldn't give a production company free rein on her land, would she? The noise alone would terrify her animals."

Mum popped the cap on her bottle of sunscreen and squirted a line along her shin. Even in autumn, the New Zealand sun could be harsh, and given that we both had the same mousy blonde hair and light skin, it seemed better to be safe than a lobster.

"I've no idea," she said, passing me the bottle. "Your

nana—God rest her soul—would have extracted every last detail from her friend by now, and no doubt they'd have cooked up some sort of plot between the two of them."

A painfully true statement. Our family had lost a huge chunk of its soul when Nana Dee-Dee unexpectedly passed last year. She'd left behind her pride and joy—Unraveled—a yarn and craft store she'd built from the ground up and which Harry had since entrusted to me. A move I know she'd have approved of.

I also appeared to have inherited the two apples of my nana's eye, jet-black kitty siblings: Kit, the chubby, food-focused boy, and Pearl, the haughty Queen of the Known Universe, prone to kleptomania. Believe me when I say they're both a joy and a pain in my rear end, but either way, I was crazy-stupid in love with them.

The pair was currently boarding at Birdie's while Harry and I were away camping. No doubt they'd have taken over the whole motel by now.

"Guess I'll find out more when I pick up the dastardly duo on Tuesday," I said.

"Found one!" my brother's voice hollered beside my ear as he thrust a foil-wrapped egg under my nose.

I jumped, my heart pounding.

Skittish? Me?

Just because I'd now twice escaped unhinged killers didn't mean I woke at every house creak late at night or leaped out of my skin each time an idiot like my baby brother thought it funny to sneak up on me.

Quick as a striking snake, I snatched the egg from his hand.

"Hey!" he grumbled as I deftly peeled off the foil and popped the chocolate into my mouth. "That was mine."

"You snooze, you lose. Loser," I said around a mouthful

of sugar as I tucked the crumpled ball of foil into the pocket of his T-shirt and smacked it flat.

Oops, my bad. He had another Easter egg in there.

I felt a satisfying crunch before caramel filling oozed out all over his shirt.

Revenge, as they say, is sweet. Especially when it's a spotless white T-shirt, and you remember the time your sibling added his new red shorts to the washing machine containing your white school blouses. Accidental, my fuzzy woolen socks.

Just goes to prove, a Wakefield never forgets...

THE CATS' dreaded pet carriers sitting on the back seat of my car, I drove the short distance out of town to where pavement turned to pastures of lush green. Cape Discovery was located in an area renowned for its orchards and vineyards. The MacKenzies had once utilized their land as an apple orchard, supplying both international and local markets. But since Birdie lost her husband, Samuel, three years ago, the orchard had become more of a liability than a viable business.

Once I'd driven through the gateway and latched it behind me—while she kept the cats in a secured enclosure, some of Birdie's rescue animals lived free range—I continued up the long driveway to the farmhouse. Birdie stood in her front yard, and I could hear her scolding someone, or something, lurking in the shrubbery. I parked in one of the designated visitors' spots and climbed out, spotting the scoldee among the rhododendrons. A bored-looking ginger tom.

One hand planted on the hip of her apple-green dungarees, Birdie used the other to wag a finger at the animal, who yawned in response. "You can deny it until the cows come home, Cheddar, but I know it was you who dug up my seedlings."

Here's a fun fact about Nana Dee-Dee's friend: she understands cats.

Now you're most likely thinking, 'of course the woman understands cats; she owns a cattery.' Nope, not what I mean. Birdie understands what cats are saying...or meowing, chirping, yowling, as the case may be. Sometimes, she once confided to my nana, they didn't even have to open their furry little mouths for her to know exactly what's going on inside their heads.

Some kind of feline mind meld? Goodness knows.

But the seventy-something widow doted on her 'guests,' and I'd no hesitation in leaving my two in Birdie's care. If nothing else, at least the duo wasn't rampaging the town's streets in my absence. Which, given the slightest encouragement, they were prone to do.

By the time I'd removed both carriers from my car, Birdie had scooped Cheddar into her arms, where he lay on his back, legs salaciously akimbo while she scratched his belly. Between his orange striped fur and Birdie's fluorescent green dungarees and matching gumboots—not to mention the bright streaks of lime coloring her otherwise gray hair—the pair were so bright that I was thankful I'd worn sunglasses.

"Hi, Birdie." I walked toward her and the blissed-out, purring cat. "Cheddar up to his old tricks?"

"That he is." Birdie kissed the tip of one ginger ear and set him down on his paws. He let out a short, chirping mew and sauntered off in the direction of the barn-like structure a short distance from the farmhouse. "Don't take that tone with me, young man," she said to his sashaying rear. "You're lucky to get any sort of belly rub after what you did to my poor seedlings."

"I hope Kit and Pearl behaved themselves," I said as we walked toward the cattery, our feet crunching over the gravel driveway.

"Perfect little darlings, as always." She offered to carry one of the carriers for me and swung it with an ease that demonstrated how strong she still was despite her small, wiry frame. Then again, the day-to-day work involved in caring for all her various animals would keep her fit regardless of her age.

Birdie's Clowder Motel was, in fact, a converted barn that had once stored the heavy machinery Samuel used to maintain their apple orchards. However, after experiencing a number of lucrative years, Samuel had built a bigger and better structure closer to the actual orchards. According to Nana Dee-Dee, Birdie had always surrounded herself with an abundance of cats, either her own or strays or those belonging to friends who asked if she could feed their pets while they were away. When Samuel made the decision to build a new barn, he'd surprised her with plans to turn the old one into a cat boardinghouse.

Now the airy space was an indoor area with separated cupboard-sized suites, suitable for a solitary cat to bunk down in for the night, and larger, closet-sized enclosures for cats belonging to the same family. As Kit and Pearl fitted this description, they had their own spot they returned to each night.

The interior also contained a large exercise area with high places to sit and observe, staged tree branches to climb, tunnels and hiding places, and windows to look out of. It was basically the feline equivalent of Disneyland, and when the weather was fine, the cats had a completely fenced-in yard to explore.

It was a beautiful autumnal morning, the sun filtering through the russet leaves of the gracious old oak trees lining the driveway, so I expected the cats would be outside. Sure enough, Pearl sat on one of the perches mounted on the barn wall, staring intently down at me. She nimbly jumped from shelf to shelf until reaching ground-level, where she disappeared into a patch of grass Birdie allowed to grow long for the cats' hiding pleasure. Kit, on the other hand, was nowhere to be seen. Since the plumper of the two kitties would've already devoured his morning kibble, I could almost guarantee he'd be off having a nap attack in a nice sunny spot. At least he'd be glad to see me.

"What's the bet Pearl will snub me for at least half a day?" I asked.

"She says you should have taken her camping as your secret weapon on the Easter egg hunt. She's quite talented at finding things, you know."

"Oh, I do know. A few weeks ago, she found a new 'toy' inside someone's handbag during the Crafting for Calmness class." I paused for dramatic effect, watching Birdie's eyes twinkle as she tried to guess what the mischievous Pearl might have discovered. "She dragged it out and proceeded to chase it across the floor. It was a tampon. Poor Harry claims he's scarred for life."

"Oh my word." Birdie clapped a hand across her mouth but failed to stop the giggles from escaping. "The naughty minx didn't share *that* story."

I grinned at her. "Please don't tease her about it. I think she's embarrassed."

"Wouldn't dream of it."

As soon as Birdie opened the barn door, bangs and

crashes assaulted my ears. I glanced around, trying to locate the source of the racket. Birdie's nephew, Dominic MacKenzie, stomped around the open enclosures, dumping used kitty litter into a wheelbarrow and tossing the plastic trays onto the floor to rinse. With his forehead creased into deep furrows that laddered up to his hairline, his scowl would have soured a saucer of milk. He wore coveralls and gumboots, and a swimmer's nose clip pinched his nostrils shut, even though I could detect no smell of cat pee. He didn't notice us at first, likely because of the headphones clamped to his ears. His every movement shouted how much he disliked doing this particular job.

Birdie obviously caught my expression. "We lost a couple of our volunteers once the high school and university kids went back, so Dominic's kindly picked up some of the slack."

Kindness didn't appear to be one of her nephew's traits. Not that I'd met the man, except for his grunt of a greeting when I dropped the cats off five days ago. Barely making eye contact as I filled out the paperwork, he hadn't even offered any assistance as I trudged back and forth from the car, lugging one cat at a time in their carriers.

Dominic was the son of Samuel's brother, and five years ago, he'd moved from Australia to help his aunt and uncle on the property. I wasn't sure of much more than that because saying Bridget's nephew wasn't chatty was an understatement.

"He doesn't look to be in a very good mood," I said out of the corner of my mouth.

"Don't mind him," she said. "He's just grumpy in the hours between me making him coffee at breakfast and bringing him a beer after dinner." With a chuckle, she set the carrier beside the closed door that led into the fenced yard.

Sounded like *the* worst housemate *ever* if you asked me. But I kept this opinion to myself as he was, after all, Birdie's only family.

I set the second carrier beside the first and swung open its latch. On the snuggly fleece blanket lining the inside, I strategically placed a few kitty treats. This was, as you might've guessed, Kit's. One merely had to leave its door open with food inside for Kit to enter like a lamb.

"While I go fetch him," Birdie said, "you come up with a plan as to how we're going to catch his feisty sister."

"Maybe if you sweet-talk her, she'll be more amenable to me transporting her home."

"I shall promise her you'll give her extra treats and a can of tuna for tea."

Pearl was definitely the trickier prospect. With her, it involved getting all five flailing appendages—four of them tipped with razor-sharp claws—into a carrier without becoming a human scratching post. Birdie slipped through the door into the yard while I fussed with Pearl's carrier, arranging her soft blanket just so.

As I crouched on the floor, a shadow fell over me. A shadow that blocked the light streaming through the high windows and filled my nostrils with a toxic combination of cologne and body odor.

I squinted up at Dominic, headphones hooked around his neck and lips curled in a sneer. "My aunt's losing her marbles. You shouldn't be encouraging her to live in some Dr. Doolittle fantasy world."

"I didn't think I was." I frowned. "And saying she's losing her marbles is kind of harsh, isn't it? She's just a tad eccentric."

"*Eccentric?* Is that what they're calling the elderlies' mental decline nowadays?"

I opened my mouth, then snapped it shut, having no idea how to respond. After all, I'd only seen Birdie once or twice since returning to Cape Discovery last year—Dominic saw her every day. Guess he'd have a better idea of his aunt's mental capabilities.

"Sorry," I said.

He gave me a curt nod before stalking back to the wheelbarrow, snapping the headphones over his ears as he went.

Birdie reappeared, Kit purring against her shoulder, his eyes sitting half-mast in feline bliss. My conscience twinged as it hit me that I should have made more of an effort to reconnect with one of Nana Dee-Dee's special friends. "Birdie, we've missed you in the Crafting for Calmness group. Would you like to join us this Thursday evening?"

Her smile faltering, she glanced past my shoulder to where her nephew was pushing the wheelbarrow out of the barn. "Oh. I don't know, honeybunch. Dominic doesn't approve of me driving at night."

Birdie set Kit on his feet. Straight away, he sniffed the air and made a beeline for his carrier.

"No problem. I'll pick you up and drop you off again afterward."

"Are you sure? I wouldn't want to be a burden."

"It'd be my pleasure," I said as crunching sounds came from inside the carrier. I latched the door behind Kit and prepared to tackle the little madam that was his sister.

Good deed done for the day?

Check.

TWO

Birdie MacKenzie slotted back into the chaos that was Crafting for Calmness like a foot into a sock. One knitted from the finest possum-merino blend yarn, of course. Although Birdie was, in fact, a proud crocheter and part of the deviousness behind a subgroup of class members who'd nicknamed themselves the Happy Hookers.

Mary Hopkins, another rebel hooker, crowed with delight when she saw her old cohort in Unraveled's workroom. "Birdie! About time you returned to the fold, my dear." She hurried to sit beside her friend, husband Gerald trailing behind, her large craft bag slung over his arm.

A few of our newer members hadn't met Birdie. Skye Johnson, the new hairstylist, for one, but they bonded immediately over their shared love of brightly colored hair dye.

The longtime regulars, however, were all excited to see her. Except, perhaps, Beth Chadwick. I suspect Beth considered she already filled the role of *Older Widow with a Shot at Relieving Harry of His Widowerhood*. Not that my granddad was having a bar of it. Or her. Clad in a shapeless floral dress suitable for a nineteen-twenties play—assuming the wardrobe mistress had zero taste and was the vindictive sort—Beth took one look at her imagined love rival and pouted. Her pout shifting to a scowl as she was forced to sit at the opposite end of the worktable since Birdie had secured the coveted spot next to Harry.

As usual, Pamela Martin, another of our regulars, was fashionably late, in keeping with her Chic Threads clothing boutique two doors down from Unraveled. She swept into the room and air-kissed my cheek, apparently having decided I was worthy of her approval after I'd somehow found myself in the middle of her family dramas this past February.

"Tessa, darling," Pamela cooed. "Any news on the Oliver front?" Spoken at a volume that carried her words to the ears of everyone already seated around the worktable.

Twelve pairs of inquisitive eyes swiveled in my direction, everyone eager for an update on my love life. One that may or may not involve an attractive pub owner called Oliver Novak. Since our embarrassing encounter on Valentine's Day, when Oliver claimed he'd ask me out on a date in due course, nothing further had eventuated.

Honestly, I couldn't blame him. Not with the likes of Pamela Martin and my mother watching and evaluating his every move. No wonder we'd both kept our distance over the past few weeks. At least, that's what I told myself as my phone slowly starved for want of a text message from the man.

Or any man, for that matter.

I pasted on my best *I Am Woman, Hear Me Roar* smile. "Nope. And contrary to what anyone else might think"— Mum, for starters—"I'm perfectly happy being single. Oliver and I are just friends."

Were we though? Were we even friends? I had my doubts. Didn't mean I intended to air those doubts in front of the voracious-for-gossip class members.

"You tell him, sister," Nadia said.

One of our newer members, who'd recently graduated from the Tuesday evening beginners group, Nadia was a uni student currently home on Easter break. "Don't let one of these silence your inner goddess." She held up her hands to show the group the latest flesh-colored, tubular creation dangling from her needles.

Nadia's latest campaign—yarn bombing her patriarchal university with knitted male genitalia—appeared to be going well.

My inner goddess chose to dismiss the flicker of hurt at Oliver's continued radio silence and instead focus on the cupcakes, sweet slices, and savory mini quiches in the center of the worktable. "Hasn't Rosie done an outstanding job with the catering this week?" I asked the group.

My former high school nemesis and current fledgling friend had decided that since I'd kinda saved her baby brother in February's dramafest, the least she could do was provide free goodies for Unraveled's twice-weekly classes. Of course, the crafters adored the different treats, so Rosie's café, the Daily Grind, benefited from follow-up orders. Win-win for the business-savvy Rosie Cooper.

A chorus of 'oohs' and 'aahs' rippled around the table as everyone interpreted my comment as a suggestion they help themselves. While they loaded up their plates, I retreated to the kitchen area and switched on the kettle for tea and coffee. By the time I returned to the table with the tray of hot drinks, the conversation had moved on from the banoffee cupcakes with a delicate toffee web decoration to Pavlova Productions.

"But isn't it something you should seriously consider, Bridget?" Pamela—never, ever *Pam*—dabbed a paper napkin to her lips. "Even with Dominic doing his best with the orchard, surely you can't continue to run the cattery and shelter alone for much longer?"

"I'm not running it alone," Birdie said. "I have volunteers who help in the shelter, and the cats mostly look after themselves." She dipped her chin toward the chair I'd vacated and Pearl, who hadn't hesitated in stealing the pre-warmed spot. "Perfect example. As long as they're fed, have fresh water and a clean litter box, they're content to do their own thing."

"What Pamela's too polite to say," Beth piped up, "is that you've reached your best-by date. You should be bending over backward to get Pavlova to pick your property. Take the money, leave your nephew to run things, and go on one of them 'golden oldies' cruises to the tropics."

While Beth had all the tact of a dump truck reversing over your foot, she and Pamela did have a point. Birdie could use an extra set of hands at the Clowder Motel. And if she couldn't find those hands, at some stage in the not too distant future, she had some hard decisions coming her way. A cushion of money from a production company might take the sting out of having to loosen her grip on the reins.

"Has someone from Pavlova Productions been to see you, Birdie?" I carefully lifted Pearl and transferred her onto my lap as I eased into my chair.

"A couple of slick city fellas showed up over the long weekend," she said. "One of them had fancy suede boots on. Didn't look so fancy after he'd traipsed around the back paddocks with Dom."

Harry chuckled and gently elbowed her arm. "Step in some animal topdressing, did he?"

"That he did. And swore a blue streak from what I heard. He hightailed it to the house while Dom and the other bloke, who'd sensibly borrowed a spare pair of gumboots, carried on. I made him a nice cuppa while we waited for the other two to return. He mentioned the main barn and the shelter being an issue for the set, said they'd want to relocate them to another site." She gave an indignant huff. "According to him, Dominic suggested they demolish both buildings and be done with it."

I wasn't the only one who sucked in a shocked breath. Anyone who knew Birdie knew how much the motel and shelter meant to her.

"Well, I hope you gave him a piece of your mind," Mary spluttered. "What a preposterous idea."

Birdie's streaky green bun jiggled as she nodded. "Oh my word, I most certainly did. Alpaca poo on his boots was the least of his worries once I'd finished with him. I told him it was my home and my land, and he'd never get my permission for Pavlova Productions to step foot on it again."

"Why did you allow them to look in the first place?" Beth asked.

"First I knew about it was my nephew introducing them when their posh SUV drove up," Birdie said with a shrug. "Dom said they might want to do some filming there, and they'd pay well for the privilege. I couldn't see any harm in having a few actors running around the apple trees, but that's not what they're wanting at all."

"More like that Hobbit movie-set place up north with truckloads of tourists visiting every day?" Gerald said. "The family that owns the farmland have done very well for themselves out of the arrangement—very well indeed."

Pamela leaned forward, dollar signs popping up in her

eyes. "How much do you think that sort of arrangement would be worth?"

"Millions," Gerald said. "If Pavlova Productions' movie ends up with a cult following like those Tolkien movies did, the sky's the limit."

"If *you* choose to look a gift horse in the mouth," Beth said, "I can guarantee someone else in Discovery will be only too happy to sign on the dotted line."

"Like your neighbor Marcus Hall," Harry said.

"Good for him, I say." Birdie turned a flinty but not unkind gaze on him. "But it's not for the MacKenzies. Over my dead body will anyone get their hands on my land."

As the conversation moved on to other topics and needles and hooks continued in motion, I couldn't help but wonder what kind of can of worms this production company might've opened.

BY THE TIME I herded Birdie into my car for the return drive home, it was almost ten. She was the last class member to leave, either not noticing or choosing to ignore my not-so-subtle yawns signaling I was ready to call it a night. However, she'd purchased a small fortune in yarn to crochet sweaters for her rescue pups, so I wasn't about to complain.

As the headlights swept over the winding two-lane country road and the scattering of cattle dozing in fields, Birdie remained suspiciously quiet, making me question if she might have dozed off. But no. As the lights from a car heading in the opposite direction washed over us, I noted Birdie sitting stiffly upright in the passenger seat.

Once I'd opened, driven through, and closed the MacKenzies' driveway gate—the bane of rural living—we continued on, gliding through pewter moonlight toward the farmhouse. Most of its windows were dark apart from a room at the front of the house. The living room drapes remained open to the night while flickering images chased each other across an enormous screen mounted on the wall.

While parking my car, I slid Birdie a side-eye. She stared straight ahead, unblinking, fingers gripping the handle of the wicker basket she used to carry her craft supplies.

My hand that had pulled on the parking brake stilled. "Is everything okay? You look...unsettled."

Without taking her eyes off the living room window, she said, "No need to worry about me. I'm hunky-dory." She dragged her gaze away from the windshield and looked over at me. "Just a little tired. It's been a while since I've socialized."

"We loved having you there tonight. I hope you'll join us again next week."

Her gaze darted back to the window and the rugby match taking place onscreen. "That would be lovely, but I can't make any promises."

"I'm happy to pick you up and drop you off again if driving's a problem."

Seeing Birdie happy among her friends made me miss Nana Dee-Dee even more, and I knew my nana would want me looking out for one of her friends now she wasn't able to. It was worth losing some sleep to be Birdie's free taxi service.

"Oh, that's very kind, honeybunch, but I don't want to be a bother."

Bother? Burden? Twice now, she'd referred to herself using such terms. Why on earth would a woman like Birdie, who'd built a small but successful business and established a volunteer-based charity for animals, feel like a burden to anyone? A prickling unease burrowed under my scalp. Maybe the problem wasn't so much a 'why' as a 'who.'

"Are you and Dominic getting on all right, living under the same roof?"

"It's nice to have someone other than me rattling around the house," she said. "Once the shock of losing Samuel wore off, I was dreadfully lonely."

Which didn't answer my question. "Is he good company for you, then?"

"He's family." Again, not quite answering my question. "It was sweet of Dominic to give up his apartment in town and move into one of his dotty aunt's spare rooms." She gave a self-deprecating laugh. "I can't imagine living with an old duck like me does much for his personal life. He's never once brought a girl home. Of course, the modern thing with young people nowadays is to woo each other online, isn't it?"

"I suppose it is." Not that Dominic would be considered a young person by any stretch of the imagination. The man was at least my age—mid-thirties—and, donning my judgy-pants, I couldn't imagine the man 'wooing' anyone. Objectively, with all his hair and his teeth intact, Dominic MacKenzie wasn't unattractive as such. I'm sure his rough-around-the-edges, wiry farmer's physique would be a drawing card for some women.

Until he opened his mouth and his personality fell out.

"But you said he doesn't approve of you going out at night?"

She sighed. "My vision's not what it used to be. He's right—I shouldn't be driving at night. Truth be told, I probably shouldn't be driving in daylight either, even with my specs on; I'm better off staying at home like he says."

Where she'd remain isolated from her community, her only daily contact with Dominic and brief interactions with clients picking up and dropping off their pets. But that was just my suspicion, not a certainty.

I opened my car door. "I'll give you a hand to carry in your yarn."

Birdie chuckled. "I did go overboard, didn't I? Bought half your stock."

"Nearly, but I'm not complaining!"

I loaded up my arms with the three shopping bags from the back seat. By the time I'd hip-bumped the door closed and made it around to the other side of the car, Birdie was already halfway to the house. Sensor lights blinked on, lighting the way as I caught up with her. She opened the door and stepped inside, softly calling her nephew's name as she peered around the living room doorway. In that moment, with her bottle-green cardigan and brown pants, she reminded me of a shy turtle stretching its neck out from the safety of its shell. Unsure whether friend or foe awaited.

Heat punched my gut and continued upward to inflame my cheeks. My nana's friend was more than unsettled—entering her own home made her anxious.

No noise came from the living room; the TV was muted.

Birdie turned to me with a frown. "Dom's not there. He should be there on the couch."

My forehead creased at the uplifted note of bewilderment in her voice. I set down the bags of yarn next to her craft basket in the hallway and joined her in peering into the living room. My gaze swept around, past a pair of armchairs that matched a two-seater sofa, to a leather recliner couch with a well-worn, butt-sized groove in one of its black cushions. The couch matched nothing else in the room, so most likely furniture Dominic brought with him when he moved. In the couch's center, a fold-down cup holder/tray held three beer bottles, a bucket-sized bowl of popcorn (a scattering of smooshed kernels on the carpet below), and two remotes.

Quite the 'single guy with no responsibilities' setup.

"He's probably stepped out for a bathroom break," I said.

But even as the words left my lips, the house strained with silence. Out here, with no neighbors close by and in a home as old as this one, there should've been some sounds: plumbing complaining, floorboards creaking, or—heaven forbid, if he was anything like my brother—the noises associated with not closing the toilet door properly while using it. Because nothing says 'I'm the king of my castle' like peeing loud enough for the entire household to hear.

A tentative mew came from a gap beneath a free-standing bookshelf, followed by scratching sounds.

"Cheddar?" Birdie moved across the room. "How'd you get yourself jammed in there?"

Another muffled cry before the ginger tom's head poked out from the space, closely followed by the rest of him as he wriggled and contorted his furry body free. Birdie snatched up the cat and wrapped him in her arms, rubbing her nose behind his ears. "Did something frighten you, silly boy?"

Continuing to croon reassurances to the cat, Birdie lifted her face from his fur. A red smear streaked her skin from nose to cheek. Nosebleed being my initial thought, I dug in my jeans pocket for a tissue.

"You've got a bit of a, a...oh..." Close enough to pass her the tissue, I realized the blood wasn't oozing from either of her nostrils.

It came from the dark-red damp patches of fur on Cheddar's head.

"What's the matter? You look like you've seen a ghost." Her arms tightened around the cat, who yowled and fought his way free. After landing on the floor with a thud, he took off like a furry orange bullet.

Neither of us had looked down when we entered the room, but tracking the cat's mad dash for freedom, my gaze skipped across the floor. Brown smears and paw prints marred the hardwood.

Red paw prints.

"There's blood on his fur," I said. "He must be hurt."

Birdie's hand flew to her throat. "Oh, the poor lamb! Tessa, can you run into the laundry room through there and bolt the cat door shut? I won't see him until morning if he escapes outside. I'll check his favorite hiding place, under my bed."

Her nephew temporarily forgotten, Birdie hurried into the hallway, hollering the cat's name and flipping on lights as she went. I dashed in the opposite direction, through the archway into her kitchen. Shadows and gloom greeted me with only the living room lights behind me as guidance, but if I wanted to foil Cheddar's escape, I had no time to scour the walls for switches. Using countertop edges as a reference, I fumbled my way across the kitchen to a cracked-open door. Cracked enough for a cat to squeeze through.

While shoving it wide with one hand, I twisted around to locate the laundry light switch with the other. Uncharacteristically for me, I found it without giving the wall an intimate pat-down, and cold white light blasted the room. Gaze fixed on the cat door, I heroically rushed to latch it, instinctively avoiding more dark brown smears on the floor. If Birdie was anything like my mum, Dominic would soon be getting a flea in his ear for messing up her otherwise pristine laundry room floor with his muddy gumboots.

Cat flap bolted shut, I whirled into a crouched defensive position in case Cheddar was hot on my heels. "No Houdini-ing on my watch, buddy."

But instead of a scared and potentially wounded kitty, beyond and partially hidden by the flung-open laundry door was said kitty's litter box.

And face down in it—sprawled on top of a spreading pool of blood—Dominic MacKenzie.

THREE

Like some kid playing 'statues,' I turned to stone; the only moving body part was my eyes.

Which weren't *literally* moving, but you know what I mean.

Too busy internally screaming, 'is that a mohair-flecking gunshot wound in his back?' to worry about life-giving oxygen, I forgot to inhale for a dozen panicked heartbeats. The smell of blood converting to a coppery taste on my tongue, I swallowed hard and willed my nostrils to stop passing vomit signals up the line to my brain.

Don't puke, breeeathe.

Huffing in shallow breaths, I forced my spine to uncurl until, eventually, I stood. On wobbly legs. But triumphantly standing.

Elsewhere in the house, Birdie continued calling for Cheddar. From the smeared paw prints and crimson-stained trail of litter leading away from the body, I suspected the poor cat was just terrified and not actually bleeding. And speaking of bodily fluids, a nice deposit of fresh feline hairball-vomit adorned the laundry room floor.

Was that why Dominic had been in the laundry? The cynic in me doubted he knew his way around a washing machine, but the universal garbled-wracking-throaty sound of a gagging cat was guaranteed to extract anyone from the couch. Unless they enjoyed scrubbing the end result off a rug or other hard-to-clean surface. Bonus points to Cheddar for choosing linoleum.

And...I was internal-monologue panic-waffling.

What was needed right now was action rather than Muppet-flailing reaction. Narrowing my eyes in an attempt to block out some of the more gruesome details, I moved closer to Dominic—sidling around the spreading stain on the linoleum—and crouched beside him.

"Dominic?" I stage-whispered, gingerly poking a spot on his shoulder that wasn't, um, stained.

Zero response. Two fingertips pressed to his throat detected only sandpaper-rough stubble and the absence of a reassuring thud-thud-thud. Recalling past first aid classes, I moved my fingertips to his wrist. Ditto. A big fat zilch. And given that he was doing a better impersonation of a statue than I had, I also concluded that breathing in the subtle aroma of kitty pee was no longer an issue for him either.

"I've found the runaway puss," Birdie called.

Her voice sounded closer. As in, 'approaching the kitchen and the dead-as-a-doornail Dominic on the laundry room floor' closer. That spurred my jellied legs into action, and I scuttled out of the room, yanking the door shut behind me. I knew you shouldn't touch anything at a crime scene—I'd seen the TV shows and listened to my retired police officer granddad's complaints—but Birdie didn't need to be traumatized by the sight of her nephew lying dead in her cat's litter box.

The overhead lights blinked on, and despite having

come from another bright room, I squinted myopically at Birdie's silhouette.

"You shut the door. Good thinking." She bustled past me, two beer bottle necks hanging woven between the fingers of one hand and one clutched in the other.

"Birdie, I—"

"Cheddar's under my bed. He tells me he feels safe there." A gush of water from the faucet and Birdie rinsed the first bottle. "He says he isn't hurt, but being a typical male, his pride would prevent him from admitting it even if he was." Bottle number one set on the counter and the second followed it under the faucet.

Everything at a crime scene is potential evidence...

"I don't think you should—"

"But I didn't come down in the last rain shower, no sir," Birdie continued as if I hadn't spoken. "I got the flashlight I keep in my nightstand for emergencies and checked him out as best I could."

Bottle number two rinsed, and before I could attempt another intervention, she'd switched to filling bottle number three. I guess what Dominic was drinking prior to taking a swan-dive into kitty litter wasn't so important in the scheme of things.

"And he doesn't appear to be bleeding. It's very strange," she concluded.

Not so strange considering what lay behind *door number one*. "Birdie, please. I need to tell you something about Dominic, and you should probably sit down while I do."

Birdie set the two now-empty bottles beside the first and wiped damp fingers on a kitchen towel. Her face crumpled as she wrung the cotton fabric in her hands. "Oh dear. Did you go into the toilet off the laundry room? Dominic uses that one, and I apologize for the dreadful state he leaves it in. The man wouldn't know a toilet brush if someone bashed him over the head with it."

"That's not it—please, come and sit down." I slipped an arm around her shoulders and led her to a seat at her kitchen table.

Something in my voice must've gotten through to her because she sank into the chair while continuing to twist the towel. I took a seat beside her and placed my hands over hers to still them. "Nana Dee-Dee always said one should deliver the truth plainly, not dress it up with little white lies, so I'll respect you both by being straight up with you now."

Her hands trembled in mine like she already knew what I was about to say. Perhaps feline minds weren't the only ones she could read.

"Dominic's in your laundry. I suspect he's been shot, and...and I'm almost certain he's dead. I'm so sorry."

Birdie's hands stopped shaking, the towel fluttering to the floor between us. Her mouth worked as if she wanted to debate the logic of coming home from a fun evening with friends to violation and violence. Things like this didn't happen in small-town New Zealand.

Except, in my experience, they did.

Her forehead an accordion of deep grooves, Birdie shuddered a breath. "Someone shot my nephew?" She gripped the table edge, half-rising from her seat.

I rocketed to my feet and put my hands on her shoulders to press her back firmly but gently toward the chair. "You can't go in there. I'm sorry, but you can't."

She didn't fight me but dropped into her chair again. "Are you sure Dominic's dead? Maybe he just, I don't know, drank too much and fell over. My nephew does enjoy a bit of tipple before going to bed."

Fairly confident a tipple or two or even three wasn't responsible for Dominic's untimely shuffle off this mortal coil, I shook my head. "I can't be sure a gun was involved because I've never seen anyone who's been killed by a firearm, but it's, ah, messy. That's how Cheddar must've gotten blood on his fur."

"Oh my word—the poor darling. No wonder he's hiding; he must've seen the whole thing. I should go ask him..." Once again, she braced her hands on the table, about to rise and interrogate the furry witness.

Once again, I stopped her. "I'm going to call the police, then we'll drive down to the gate and wait for them to arrive."

"We will? Why can't we just stay here with Cheddar and put the kettle on?"

"We can't risk contaminating the crime scene any further." With a firm grip on her elbow, I helped her to her feet and escorted her back into the living room.

"Like *CSI: NY*," Birdie said. "I do love that Gary Sinise, don't you? Such a handsome young man."

As we passed what I'd mentally labeled 'Dominic's Throne,' I couldn't help but study the area where he'd sat. Next to the couch stood a side table cluttered with assorted man-junk, two disconnected charging cords hanging over its edge. No sign of the devices they belonged to.

"I tried *CSI: Miami* for a while." Birdie tugged on my arm to get my attention as we continued on out of the house. "But the lead reminded me too much of that William Shatner bloke. Him, I don't like."

While Birdie critiqued the former *Star Trek* captain's acting skills, or lack thereof, I guided her over to my car, helped her into the passenger seat, and clipped the seat belt into place. Once I'd shut the door, I called emergency services and gave the operator the MacKenzies' address. As I babbled away to the patient man safely ensconced in a building somewhere a gun-toting killer wasn't, non-temperature-related heat flooded through me. Feeling both sweaty and clammily chilled, I glanced about with eyes peeled for danger.

An idea galloping around in my brain but not yet fully formed made getting away from the house vitally important. And not only because it would make a certain detective sergeant hopping mad if I once again messed with a crime scene.

No. While the operator advised that 'a car is being dispatched to your location' and instructed me to 'stay on the line'—or words to that effect; I was too focused on trying to activate my night vision—I could think of only one thing.

What if the gunman's still around?

SOMETHING YOU MIGHT NOT KNOW about the New Zealand Police: when one reports the involvement of a firearm in an incident, they dispatch a specialist force of armed officers. With their head-to-toe black Kevlar, helmets, and massive weapons, those guys are big, bad, and scary. So picture Birdie's and my shocked expressions when, a relatively short time after I'd made the call, half a dozen of these guys and gals descended on the MacKenzie property.

To quote Birdie: *Oh my word.*

While they searched, we waited at the bottom of the driveway with the local constabulary, who'd arrived just before them. In a cordoned-off area, Birdie and I huddled in a police car with the heater blasting.

"I feel like a criminal." Her nose pressed to the window,

Birdie watched the comings and goings outside. "Why couldn't we stay in your car?"

"I'm not sure, but at least it's nice and warm in here." I glanced at my phone, which had been blowing up with concerned messages from Harry, my parents, and Rosie—her most recent making me grimace, shiver, and blush in rapid succession.

ROSIE: Has your yummy detective from Napier arrived yet? Silver lining, eh?

THE DETECTIVE she referred to was none other than Detective Sergeant Eric Mana. And, mmm, he sure was easy on the eye. With a physique of a professional-level rugby player and the dress sense of a well-appointed businessman, Eric Mana was, in a word, yummy.

Of course, it would take the entire unit of armed officers acting as a firing squad before I'd admit it.

A quick glance out my side of the car revealed the arrival of a dark SUV, one of the local officers bending down to the vehicle's open window to chat.

ME: Just shown up. Wish me luck. He won't be pleased to see me.

AND JUDGING by the scowl on his face as he emerged from the SUV, someone had already informed him that his least favorite witness was once again in the wrong place at the wrong time.

Gimme a break. It wasn't like I ran around offing people for a further opportunity to admire his brooding good looks. His black would-curl-if-any-longer hair. His gray eyes—the color of sea fog one moment and the next, unyielding steel. His firm jaw and the distinctive chiseled features of his Māori heritage. And the charisma he wore casually, the way some men could don old jeans and a leather jacket and make your knees weaken.

My phone pinged.

ROSIE: Just be yourself and you'll be fine. Scratch that. Be someone who isn't awkward and prone to embarrassing encounters with men.

I RESPONDED with a rude emoji then flicked my phone to mute. The last thing I needed was a distraction when talking to the detective. What I actually needed was a convenient person to run interference, but I'd settle for not making an idiot of myself. Again.

Not wanting Birdie to overhear me receiving a dress down, I climbed out, shut the door, and waited. Probably should've been more patient, as by the time he'd finished talking to the officer in charge, I was shivering.

A fingernail tapped on the window behind me, interrupting my admiration of how Eric rocked a pinstripe suit and managed to look daisy-fresh even this close to midnight. Whereas I most likely resembled Cinderella's after-midnight attire, once everything reverted to pumpkins and field mice.

When Birdie gave up tapping and rapped on the glass instead, I turned around and dipped my head.

"Find out when I can go back up, will you?" she asked at a volume that suggested a soundproof wall between us rather than a car window. "I want to make sure the animals are all right."

"They'll be fine, but I'll find someone in charge to ask."

"What about that fella?" She pointed to a spot beyond my shoulder. "He looks like someone who'd know."

I didn't need a visual to confirm which fella she meant.

"Ooh." Her eyebrows arched up toward her green-streaked bangs. "That one's a bit of a hunk, isn't he?"

Once more, no need for visual confirmation of who Birdie was eyeballing.

"Birdie," I hissed, "kinda inappropriate given the circumstances."

Her eyebrows drooped. In fact, her whole face sagged, instantly adding twenty years to her demeanor. And as her eyes grew shiny with tears, I wished I could take back my words. What was the harm in allowing her a harmless distraction from her grief and worries?

I pressed my palm to the glass. "I'm sorry."

"As am I to find you in such unfortunate circumstances once again," came Eric's voice from close behind me.

Offering Birdie a reassuring smile, I took my sweet time turning to face him.

You don't call; you don't write...

Or maybe *So, we meet again, mwhahahaha.*

I settled for a cucumber-cool, "Good evening, Detective. How are you tonight?" Two could play his über-formal 'I'm the law; you're a civilian' game.

"Busy. Stressed. Inconvenienced. Take your pick."

Inconvenienced by being called away from...a hot date? Couldn't help but be curious whether Eric Mana actually *did* date. However—speaking of inappropriate—now was not the time to be pondering such things. Because, *hello*, a man had died.

"Have they found anyone during their search?"

"No." He cocked his head to one side and gave an eyebrow lift of acknowledgment to the car's rear window. "Mrs. MacKenzie, we can't allow you to return home just yet. One of our officers located a cat—"

Birdie cracked open the door. "That'd be Cheddar. He'll be traumatized by all these strangers stomping around the house."

"According to the officer who took care of him, Cheddar's fed and contained in one of your cattery cages. We've also taken care of your other animals and will continue to do so until you're able to return."

"And when will that be?"

"Tomorrow morning at the earliest. You won't be going home tonight."

She sputtered a string of 'buts.'

"My parents have insisted you stay with them," I said. "So I'll drop you off at their place tonight and pick you up again in the morning to help with the animals."

"Oh." Birdie deflated, huddling into the back seat. "All right then. You're a sweet girl, Tessa. Thank you."

"We'll look after you, don't you worry. Now shut the door, or you'll get cold."

Once the door clunked shut, I returned my attention to the detective. "Do you need my full statement tonight? Or can it wait until tomorrow?"

When he angled his head away from the car in a 'let's walk over there' gesture, I strode off toward the spindly silhouettes of breeze-blown trees and another driveway belonging to the neighboring property. The driveway wound up through a copse of trees hiding the palatial home of Marcus Hall from the main road. No expense had been spared on the landscaped edges, which stood in sharp contrast to the insidiously spreading weeds and overgrown shrubs bordering the MacKenzies'.

However, despite the immaculately groomed Hall property entrance and the clouds parting to reveal a full moon, I still managed to stumble over an uneven patch of gravel. Strong fingers gripped my elbow, preventing me from rolling into a roadside ditch like some drunken cow after a weekend bender. Having not realized how closely Eric was walking beside me, I started. He either didn't notice or pretended not to, continuing to grip my elbow lightly until we reached relatively clumsy-oaf-proof solid ground.

Once confident I was no longer at risk of falling flat on my face, he released my arm and turned to me. "A formal statement tomorrow is fine. You know how it works."

I did indeed. But I chose to ignore his implication I was jinxed or in league with the Grim Reaper. "You want the Cliffs Notes version?"

"Yes."

"Was Dominic MacKenzie shot?"

He slid a sideways glance across to where a carnival-like crowd of media and people-who'll-rubberneck-at-car-crashes huddled beyond the blocked-off section of road.

"Everyone'll know sooner or later," I said helpfully. Then, as his steely gaze twitched back to mine, I hastily added, "Not from me, of course."

Eric sighed. "He was shot. Three times."

With a wince, I shoved my fists into my jacket pockets. "Poor Birdie. I'm glad I was there tonight; it would have been awful for her to see her nephew like that."

"I'm sorry you had to." His voice had gentled into a rough grumble, and call me delusional, but I could have sworn I detected more than just professional concern in his tone. And believe me, that rattled me almost much as a dead body in kitty litter.

"Unfortunately, it's kind of my signature thing now." I gave an awkward little snort of a chuckle then launched into the latest installment of *How Tessa Found a Corpse*.

Eric had a way of focusing his attention that was almost tangible; you just knew he was genuinely listening and processing your every word. Unlike many people, he didn't interrupt while I talked. Instead, his uncanny memory recalled every single sentence, and whenever I ran out of steam, he'd nudge more clarity, more detail from me with thoughtful, insightful questions.

After two previous run-ins with the man, I didn't want to be accused of leaving out anything, so I babbled until my spit dried up. About the blood-smeared cat. About the apparently missing phone and another device, and the beer and spilled popcorn. I even included the cat vomit on the laundry room floor.

"Do you think it might be a burglary gone wrong?" I asked when an awkward silence eventually descended.

"Yet to be determined."

"For a couple of devices? Seems kinda unlikely, don't you think?" I pressed. "As far as I know, Birdie and her nephew don't own anything a thief would want."

"We haven't yet had sufficient time to conduct a thorough search of the property or to obtain an inventory of the house's contents from Mrs. MacKenzie."

The detective sergeant was back in this chilly-smooth voice, the one I knew—from past experience—he switched to when he'd decided any further information was on a need-to-know basis. And as a civilian, I didn't need to know.

I narrowed my eyes. "So you're telling me the residents

of Cape Discovery should be careful to lock their doors tonight?"

He gave me a bland stare. "No more than they already should. But until we figure out why Mr. MacKenzie died, I suggest you stay vigilant."

"Of course."

Detective Mana dipped his chin, the moonlight highlighting his serious expression. "And, please, stay out of trouble."

FOUR

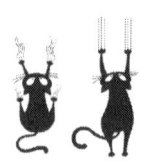

THE FOLLOWING MORNING, everyone was ecstatic to see Birdie and me.

Everyone who possessed fur and fangs, that is. Demanding meows and chirps greeted us, and felines rose on their hind legs to bat at us as we walked past their enclosures.

Police still swarmed all over the property, but at what felt like the crack of dawn, uniformed officers allowed us through the gate to tend to the animals.

An officer had thrown together a suitcase of Birdie's belongings last night, so she wore a fresh green-themed outfit this morning. Poor woman looked like she hadn't slept a wink, and even I struggled to function on the few hours uninterrupted by nightmares of someone trying to break into my room.

I worked quickly, following Birdie's instructions on freshening water and food bowls, spot cleaning litter boxes —I was a pro-level poop-scooper—and who was most likely to make a break for it while I carried out said chores. With the Easter long weekend over, only three cats remained in the Clowder Motel. Four, if you counted Cheddar, and he made it clear he didn't appreciate being lumped in with Birdie's common boarders.

By the time we'd locked the cattery behind us and headed to the smaller building attached to it, it was already mid-morning. The animal rescue shelter housed everything from hedgehogs and lost dogs to native birds that'd had a run-in with a cat and survived to tell the tale. At present, Birdie had only two rescues: a seagull with a sore wing—that I suspected was faking it for the food handouts—and a white rabbit someone had handed in on Easter Monday. Bunny and bird fed and watered, and maid service performed on their enclosures, we had one final stop. The back paddock containing the four alpacas Birdie was minding for a friend going through a messy breakup.

"All this emotional upheaval's upset the girls terribly," she confided in me as we continued along the driveway toward the newish barn that had been Dominic's domain.

At the sound of our approaching gumboot-clumpy footsteps, two police officers poked their heads out the door. One was local cop Constable Jeremy Austin, who looked more middle-aged surfer than authority figure. His partner disappeared back into the barn with a dismissive grimace once he realized it was only two harmless women.

Hah—little did he know!

I could kill him a half dozen ways with the bucket of alpaca pellets I carried. Not that I would, of course, being a law-abiding citizen and all.

Giving us a chin-lift of acknowledgment, Jeremy sauntered out of the barn. "Were you aware that there's llamas about?" he asked by way of greeting.

"They're alpacas," I said with no small amount of pride that I knew the difference—since Birdie had explained it on the walk here. And now the teacher in me delighted in passing on this snippet of trivia. "Llamas have elongated faces and large, banana-shaped ears. Whereas alpacas have shorter, blunt faces with smaller ears."

"Can't say I noticed their ears." Jeremy angled his head toward the newer barn. "But there were four of them wandering around here a few minutes ago."

Birdie's gaze darted left and right. "Oh my word! How on earth did they get out? C'mon, Tessa." She yanked on my arm and, with surprising strength, towed me at full speed around the side of the barn.

The four alpacas—two caramel-colored, one dark-chocolate brown, the other chocolate-dipped vanilla—stood huddled together by the wire fence surrounding the back paddock. Birdie sent me off in a wide circle around them to open the gate while she tempted them with the bucket's contents.

"Blanche, Dorothy, Sophia, and Rose, you beautiful, naughty girls," Birdie crooned, shaking the bucket so the pellets rattled.

Didn't take much to get the girls' attention. They trotted over to her, and like the Pied Piper, she led them toward me and the gate I was about to open.

Except it was already open.

Not much, but enough for alpacas to stroll through single file—the toe prints trampled into the mud evidence of that. As I pulled the gate wider and stood behind it on shepherding duty, I couldn't help but notice the footprints squelched deep into the mud near the post. Man-sized footprints.

The herd jostling around Birdie, she led them into the back paddock with handfuls of pellets. After following them, I closed and secured the gate behind me. In amongst the foot-traffic evidence was a couple of slick smears—as if someone wearing shoes not suitable for traipsing around farmland had slipped in the mud. A film scout in his fancy boots? But the marks looked too fresh for a tour of the property a few days ago. What about a killer running away from the crime scene? Possibly. I shivered and made a mental note to speak to Jeremy on our return trip.

"Someone left the gate open." I took a handful of pellets and offered them to the closest alpaca. Her whiskery lips tickled my palm. "And there are fresh footprints as well."

"I noticed that." Birdie lightly pushed one alpaca's face away from another that was collecting its treat from her palm. "Dominic was out here yesterday, but he knew better than to leave a gate unlatched."

Or to wear shoes in gumboot territory.

"Hello there," a man's voice called from across the field.

Marcus Hall waved at us from his side of the boundary fence, his sunbaked face creased into a deep frown beneath a battered leather outback hat.

With rotund belly straining against a flannel shirt and hanging over faded-to-gray jeans, Marcus put the middle in middle-aged. Raising the wide brim of his hat long enough to scratch his almost hairless scalp, he walked alongside the boundary fence.

If you were willing to bet against one of Cape Discovery's richest men looking like a salt-of-the-earth farmer, you'd soon lose a fortune. Marcus Hall thought dressing down, making appearances at local events, and sponsoring the town's Sunday morning farmers market made him a man of the people. Only problem was most of those people saw straight through his ruse to the ruthless businessman beneath.

Something he had in common with Rosie's father, as I'd recently discovered firsthand.

While Marcus clumped over to us in gumboots that should've been retired a generation ago, I couldn't help comparing them to the size of the prints by the gate. Hmm. Looked like he wore a similar size to me. For a big guy, Marcus had surprisingly dainty feet.

"Morning, Birdie," he hollered.

Rose, Dorothy, Sophia, and Blanche took one wide-eyed gawk at him then hotfooted it in the opposite direction. Clever girls. Empty bucket at her feet, Birdie went hands on hips and jutted out her chin. Sure didn't require my counseling degree to figure out Marcus wasn't one of her favorite people.

"You don't have to yell. I'm not deaf. And it's Mrs. MacKenzie to you, mister," she said. "Or maybe Bridget, since I did appreciate your donation to my animal rescue work at the start of the year."

A donation he'd turned into an extravaganza by presenting her with a giant check at a bake sale she'd organized. He'd gotten his picture in the local paper, grinning like he was wholly responsible for saving the whales and pandas instead of donating what was, in all likelihood, less than his weekly petrol budget.

"You're welcome, Bridget. Anything for those critters of yours."

As she harrumphed, his squinty gaze tracked over to me. "And you must be Alan's prodigal daughter. Teresa, isn't it?"

"Tessa. I'm Tessa."

Since my dad ran his own green-thumb business growing and selling fresh herbs and flowers, he'd had some dealings with Marcus over the years. As far as I was aware,

Dad avoided Marcus's hearty 'one of the boys' routine whenever their paths happened to cross, so it seemed unlikely Marcus knew the real reason I'd returned to Cape Discovery late last year. A broken heart and shattered dreams were no one's business but my own.

"What do you want, Marcus?" Birdie asked.

"I've been up in Auckland for the past couple of days—just flew in this morning, actually, only to find police and news crews swarming all over the place like flies. Soon as I found out what'd happened, I wanted to do the neighborly thing and offer my condolences on the loss of your nephew in such tragic circumstances."

"Thank you," she replied stiffly.

"In the spirit of being neighborly," I said, "it looks like the shooter might've come this way last night, probably cutting across your land to get to the main road."

Marcus twisted in the direction he'd come from, as if expecting a gunman to pop out from behind a tree. "Haven't seen any sign of him." He turned to us with a shrug. "Most likely hoisted himself over the wire and scarpered."

I followed his gaze to a section of classic Kiwi number-8-wire fencing, the posts and wire knocked wonky from what appeared to be a fair amount of traffic going over it. A strip of flattened grass on either side supported that theory. "Sure looks well used."

"The foraging group was through here in the long weekend, collecting wild fungi," Birdie said.

Marcus snorted. "I could hear Dominic going off at them about it from the house. Not to speak ill of the dead, but your nephew could be a right bully when things didn't go his way."

Birdie flinched, and her shoulders sagged. "He was

strong-willed, is all. Like his father." She shook her head sadly. "I don't know how I'll manage without him."

I slipped an arm around her shoulders. "We'll figure it out. Don't you worry."

"Perhaps you should reconsider Pavlova Productions' interest in your property, Bridget? I believe there's a lot of money on offer."

Birdie's slumped shoulders immediately straightened. "I don't want their filthy Hollywood money."

Hands raised in a *don't shoot the messenger* gesture, Marcus took a step back. "Fair enough, fair enough. It's your decision to make, after all. Stick to your guns, I say." Then, seeming to realize what he'd said, he cleared his throat while squeezing his bulbous nose. "I'll leave you to get on with it. Again, my sympathies."

"When you see that movie lot, you can tell them to take their offer elsewhere," Birdie snapped. "I won't change my mind, do you hear?"

"I hear ya," he said.

Perhaps it was my imagination or a trick of the morning light, but I could have sworn Marcus Hall's mouth curved upward in a triumphant smile as he walked away.

APART FROM A TRAVELING carnival complete with lions and tigers and bears, the next to last thing I expected to see when leaving the MacKenzies' was a picket line. But there one was just the same.

Clutching hand-painted signs on sticks and what appeared to be a king-single-size white bedsheet as a banner, the group of protesters didn't even reach double digits. But what they lacked in warm bodies, they made up for in enthusiasm. They jiggled their signs—'Movie Hacks Go Back!' 'Say NO-va to Pavlova!'—and stretched their sheet-banner: 'Keep Cape Discovery Clean and Green!' across the road. One protester brandished a megaphone while arguing with a police officer.

Birdie craned forward in the passenger seat, trying for a better view through the windshield. "Who's that pushing his luck with the boys in blue?"

I narrowed my eyes at Megaphone Man, his face partly obscured by said megaphone and the peak of a baseball cap. But I'd recognize that lank brown ponytail poking through the hole in his hat and the Ichabod Crane physique from a mile off. At closer to six-foot-six than six-foot-even, Gavin Schmidt was hard to miss. Even though he looked like the breeze scuttling pretty autumn leaves along the road could push him over.

"That's Gavin Schmidt."

I'd already come to a halt at the end of Birdie's driveway, intending to turn left toward town, but I now considered wrenching on the handbrake.

"Marcy's son who works at Sunnyville Nursing Home?" Birdie asked.

"The very one." I didn't know him well, but Sean was on friendly terms with him since they'd gone to high school together. "And he'll end up getting himself arrested if he keeps this up."

The natural mediator in me itched to intervene and calm both parties down, but I hesitated. Until I spotted someone else that I recognized among the small group of protesters. *Ah, gee whiskers.* Now I had to try. "Darn it. One of the young women you met in class last night is out there."

Birdie frowned. "Which one? The hairstylist with impeccable taste or the one knitting male appendages? She's quite talented, I have to admit. They really do look like a bloke's—"

"Nadia," I blurted. "It's Nadia. Wait here while I find out what's going on."

"Better hurry," she said. "Marcus is heading down the hill, and it looks like he's on the warpath."

Through Birdie's passenger window, I spotted him storming down his driveway.

"Sh-*Sherbe*t," I muttered and yanked on the handbrake.

As I hurried along the road verge, Nadia didn't notice me; she was too busy waving her sign and theatrically punching her fist in the air. Perhaps for the benefit of the news van that'd appeared on the other side of their picket line.

"Nadia," I stage-whispered, coming up behind her.

On hearing her name, she paused in her sign-waving and turned. Her frown turned upside down at the sight of me. "Hey! Have you come to join us?"

"Join you in doing what? Getting yourself arrested?" I shot a glance at Gavin and the Hi-Vis vested officer.

Fortunately for him, the female officer looked young enough to be fresh out of police college and, therefore, had the patience of a saint. Put an experienced and consequently more 'I've had enough of your shenanigans' cop in her position, and Gavin would've been bundled off already.

Someone like a certain detective, my brain not so helpfully supplied. Few people would dare shout in his face. Although, in defense of the new recruit, she was doing brilliantly well not to snatch the megaphone out of Gavin's hands and shove it somewhere it wouldn't echo.

"We're peaceful protesters." Nadia had to raise her voice so I could hear her over the shouting. "We're not doing any harm. It's those movie people who'll harm Cape Discovery if we give them an inch."

"Yeah!" Next to her, a red-cheeked man rocking a goatee and a *Game of Thrones* T-shirt gave his sign an extra-hard shake. "Preach it, sister."

Nadia's nose crinkled as she took a disassociating sidestep away from him. She lowered her sign and gestured for me to join her a short distance away, where we'd at least be able to converse without shouting.

"Gavin reckons that if Pavlova Productions secures a location here, it'll spell long-term disaster for the environment. Hundreds of extra people will move in for goodness knows how long. Rabid fans will show up, hoping to catch a glimpse of someone famous, putting more demands on our resources, and cluttering up our streets with their trash, worse than vacationers. There'll be more trucks and buses and motor homes adding to the air pollution, not to mention the huge carbon footprint the company itself will leave—"

I held up a stop-sign palm. "Okay, okay. I get it."

Also got the distinct impression of a budding disciple quoting directly from her guru's handbook. "But is protesting this cause worth getting arrested for? Or is there another way that won't negatively impact your future?"

She gave a sulky little shrug and looked away—toward Gavin. Who had, thankfully, stopped bellowing into the megaphone long enough to move himself and his two other groupies who held the banner off the road. The officer ensured they were well behind the road markings before waving past the small queue of waiting cars.

"Why are you here, anyway?" I asked her.

Nadia tore her eyes from Gavin and returned them to me, her worshiping expression morphing into a 'duh' pout.

"Because Gavin heard the location scouts from Pavlova will be here this morning."

Him again.

I saw a hand-knitted-with-love project coming his way in the not too distant future. Here's hoping it wasn't a set of anatomically correct male and female body bits. The crafters' equivalent to dick pics? I shook the image out of my head, trying to refocus on Nadia's words.

"...supports Greenpeace and Friends of the Earth... global environmental change... passionate about what he believes in...fights for the underdog...he's so good with the oldies he looks after. He's even working on an adopt a nana or poppa program for schools...just a stellar person, really. And you should consider—"

Marcus Hall's indignant shouting put an end to Nadia's glowing testimonial. A heat-seeking missile zeroing in on one particular target, he stormed past us without a glance and jerked to a halt in front of Gavin. Close enough that his belly could almost have held up the banner between them. Then, perhaps realizing his nose was level with the taller man's nipple, Marcus backed up a few steps and stabbed a finger at Gavin instead. "You and your motley crew get off my land. Right now."

"Technically, this isn't your land," Gavin said. "It's a public road, and we've every right to be here."

Marcus blustered, but before he could gather any more steam, another vehicle slowed to a standstill beside the officer. A window buzzed down, and the driver leaned an elbow on the sill to talk.

The expensive SUV's arrival shot a jolt of excitement into the gathered crowd. Protesters protested louder and more vigorously. Marcus also protested the protesters protesting more vigorously, albeit at a lesser volume. The blast of frantic energy dimming a fraction when he snatched the megaphone from Gavin's hand and hurled it into a prickly bush across the drainage ditch.

Marcus turned on his heel and marched over to the SUV, shedding his aggressive, outraged demeanor along the way, much as a snake sheds its skin. "Welcome, welcome!" he gushed to the driver as he shoved a meaty hand through the open window and shook the man's hand. After they'd exchanged a few words, Marcus slid into the vehicle's back seat and slammed the door. The SUV crept past us and turned into his driveway, Marcus's profile a picture of smugness as he said something to the driver that we weren't privy to and clapped him on the shoulder.

Much of the protestors' intensity faded once the SUV disappeared up the driveway. I squeezed Nadia's arm, told her I'd see her at class next week, and returned to my car.

Birdie sat hunched in the passenger seat when I opened the door and climbed in. She stared at me with puppy-dog eyes. "Dominic was sold on the idea of them filming the movie on our land. That boy had the gift of the gab, and if he were alive, he'd have convinced the powers that be to choose us. Marcus would've known it'd be tough to compete with Dominic's power of persuasion, especially when our ten acres is a prettier parcel of land. Do you reckon that had anything to do with what happened to my nephew?"

My hands, sitting at ten and two on the steering wheel, clenched. "Marcus told us he was up in Auckland."

Birdie harrumphed softly. "Unlike animals, honeybunch, people lie." Re-fastening her seat belt, she gave me a beatific smile. "Now, how about we make a quick stop at your pal Rosie's place and pick up something yummy for lunch? My treat."

I suspect my smile was not as sincere as hers, although

my saliva glands did perk up at the idea of a freshly baked muffin. Or three.

Directing the hood of my car toward the Daily Grind, I discovered that even images of golden-brown mounds of baked flour, sugar, butter, and eggs couldn't clear my brain of Birdie's earlier accusation.

Did I reckon Marcus Hall was a cold-blooded killer?

Hmm, perhaps?

While it wasn't exactly a denial, I couldn't let myself fall into a well of whodunit curiosity. At least, not until I was sure I could safely climb out again.

FIVE

Later that day, I killed the proverbial two birds with one stone. Okay, maybe that should be one bird, one crazy cat lady, zero stones involved, and no one died on the drive to Napier Police Station with Birdie. Whatevs, as my younger brother's fond of saying whenever I correct him on his constant idiom mix-ups.

Interview and statements out of the way—not to Detective Mana because he was out, well, detecting—Birdie and I headed home to Cape Discovery.

And this time, to her actual home, since the police were allowing her back into her house. Birdie seemed rather chipper about life 'returning to normal' and positively dreamy at the prospect of sleeping in her own bed. Goodness knows how many z's I'd catch, knowing my only living relative had met with an unfortunate end between my washer and dryer. Not many would be my guess. But crime scene cleaners had been through the house, and if that was good enough for Gary Sinise and *CSI*, then it was good enough for Bridget May MacKenzie.

We were coasting around a curve in Birdie's driveway

when I spotted someone walking up ahead of us, and as we drew closer, the person turned and waved. Dressed in cargo pants and a baggy sweatshirt, they had their hood up against the drizzle of rain but tugged it down as I braked to a halt. The woman, who looked to be in her late twenties, had pretty cinnamon-colored hair framing a heart-shaped face. Although she was a regular in the Daily Grind queue—triple-soy, no sugar, no foam latte—I recognized her face but didn't know her name.

However, Birdie did. She buzzed down the window and reached out a hand, which the woman took and squeezed affectionately. "April," Birdie said. "Don't tell me you're out foraging in this weather—you'll end up soaked through in no time."

April...foraging. My brain rifled through its memory banks and came up with April Bradford, the field-to-table foraging group's organizer, who I'd spoken to this past February, but only on the phone.

"Oh no, Birdie," she said. "I'm just coming up to see you. I was so sorry to hear about your nephew."

Yep. I didn't know her name but sure recognized that perky voice.

"Thank you. Why don't you hop in, and we'll give you a ride up to the house? I'll make us a nice cuppa."

April dipped to meet my gaze through Birdie's open window. "Is that okay? Oh, hi there—I know you from somewhere, don't I?"

I smiled at her. "I spoke to you on the phone once, and I often see you getting your caffeine fix at Rosie's."

"Ah, yes, I remember. You're Tessa Wakefield—the yarn store owner who *unravels* murder mysteries." As she chuckled at her own pun, I caught a glimpse of her teeth.

The orthodontist who'd fitted April's adult braces

should be able to spring for a luxury cruise just from her treatment alone. Crooked and overcrowded teeth fought to escape her rose-pink lips—lips that self-consciously snapped shut again.

"That's me," I said. "Hop in."

She climbed into the back seat behind Birdie, and we continued on up the driveway. Once inside, April offered to help me carry Birdie's belongings through to her bedroom while the older woman put on the kettle. After setting her bits and pieces on her bed, we found Birdie standing at her kitchen sink, arms wrapped around her waist as she stared bleakly at the laundry room door. The electric kettle remained off, so the only sound was Birdie's shuddery breaths. Maybe it was too soon for her to return home.

"I'll make the tea." I touched her shoulder, and she jumped, shooting me a glance I'd swear looked more guilty than startled.

"No need to trouble yourself," she said. "I just got a wee bit distracted." She unwound her arms from her waist and swiped her palms down her pant legs. "I could do with stretching my legs before we sit down again. How about we walk up to the barn and let poor Cheddar out? He'll be wondering what he's done to end up stuck in solitary confinement."

"Good idea," April said. "It's clearing up out there, and the fresh air will do us all good."

The rain had eased to a few errant spits, the clouds already peeling away on the horizon to reveal the blue backdrop of another clear but chilly autumn evening. As we walked three abreast along the graveled path to the barn, I daydreamed about getting home to the snuggly afghan I was knitting in brushed wool yarn.

"Watch your step!" Birdie yanked on my arm.

Glimpsing thick reddish-brown mud in front of my trip-to-the-city ankle boots, where I'd wandered too close to the path's edge, I stumble-hopped back onto more solid ground. "Whoops."

The remaining Clowder Motel occupants acted as if they hadn't seen hide nor hair of a human being for days instead of a few hours. Pitiful mews echoed around their enclosures, Cheddar being the loudest.

"It wouldn't hurt to feed them an hour earlier than usual, I suppose," Birdie said. "Want to give me a hand again, Tessa?"

"I can help too," April said. "That's another reason why I'm here. You've always been so generous, letting our group roam around your property, that I want to do something practical to help until you, ah, find a replacement for your nephew. Tessa has her store to run, haven't you?"

"Yes, but Harry's more than happy to mind it while I—"

"A short-term solution that's been most appreciated today, I'm sure." April sent me a tight-lipped smile. "But the next couple of weeks will be tough for poor Birdie, and I'm willing to do the day-to-day scutwork while she concentrates on the less pleasant aspects, such as organizing a funeral service." April all but mouthed the last two words as though Birdie were some child she didn't want to upset.

"That's kind of you to offer," said Birdie. "But won't coming up here twice a day interfere with your accounting work?"

"Anywhere there's Wi-Fi and a power outlet, I can work." April shrugged. "If I moved into your spare room for a few days, I could work *and* help you with the animals."

"I thought you didn't like cats?" Birdie asked.

"Whatever gave you that idea?" April strode over to the

nearest enclosure and waggled a finger through a gap in the wire. "I adore them. Here kitty, kitty, kitty," she crooned.

The sleek feline inhabitant flattened his ears and hissed—a sound that had April's finger returning to the safety of her body as if spring-loaded. She aimed a slit-eyed stare at the cat as he growled low in his throat and backed into a corner.

While she might adore kitties, it appeared this particular one didn't share the same sentiment. Earlier, Birdie had told me Pinto was even more highly strung than usual because his human parents had just adopted a puppy. Anyone invading his personal space was asking for feline aggression unless they took the time to chat to him from a safe distance first. A precaution I'd taken this morning, thereby not receiving such a fierce reaction when I'd approached.

Birdie's gaze zipped from the cat to April and back—almost as though she were confirming Pinto's thoughts on the matter. From the shadow of a frown on her face, she seemed to think the Abyssinian disapproved of this new volunteer, but Birdie slowly nodded her head. "If you're sure. I could use the help and company—for a few days, anyway."

"I'm positive. It's settled then." Without so much as a backward glance at the cat, April returned to us. "I'm at your disposal, Birdie. Just tell me what to do."

As April had walked to Birdie's—"Walkers gotta walk," she'd told me—I offered to drop her home. She lived in a modest little house on the outskirts of town, and on the drive there, we made listless conversation about a recently released vegetarian cookbook by a celebrity chef but exchanged no personal details.

Such as why she was so insistent on moving in with

Birdie or why she'd volunteered to help look after furry creatures that I suspected she wasn't all that fond of.

But perhaps I'd been unduly influenced by a certain suspicious-minded detective asking questions under the assumption that everyone had an ulterior motive for acts of kindness. So I merely wished her good luck and drove home.

Not being a slob, after parking my car, I leaned into the back seat to retrieve the empty muffin bag from our drive to Napier. As I did so, a couple of gravel chunks and a reddish-brown smear of drying mud on the footwell mat snagged my attention. The mud looked awfully similar to the stuff I'd nearly stumbled into up by the cattery.

Huh. April sat on that side on the way up to Birdie's. But she'd been walking *up* to the house when we met her on the driveway...hadn't she?

I sat forward again, clutching the crumpled paper bag to my chest. As my reflection frowned at me from the rearview mirror, I made a concerted effort to smooth my brow. Because *wrinkles*.

"What if April wasn't walking up the driveway but turned back toward the house when she heard my car? What if she'd been walking around the property?" I asked my reflection.

Reflection-me shrugged. There was also another perfectly logical and not-at-all-sinister explanation for the floor of my car: I'd developed an oversensitivity to mud and dirt, is all.

I mean, it seemed unlikely we'd stumbled onto April scoping out the terrain with plans to put an alpaca-napping plan into action.

Didn't it?

I SHOULD'VE LEARNED by now that anything my mother offered to 'treat' me to would either be a: mentally or physically painful, b: humiliating, or c: all of the above. But for all my education, I still hadn't learned this lesson.

And that was why I found myself lying in an uncomfortable chair on Saturday morning, staring up someone's nostrils. At least this time, it wasn't the dentist's nose. This nose had a gold stud in it and belonged to Skye Johnson.

Bent over me in her workplace—the Hair Today salon—she chatted away while massaging my scalp over the basin. Whatever coconut-fruity concoction she was rubbing into my hair caused my mouth to water, making it even harder to concentrate on her words.

Not that she was talking to me. Rather, she was engaged in an animated debate with my mum, who sat in the chair next to mine. Discussing, if you please, 'What to Do with Tessa's Unruly Mop of Curls.'

Goodness knows, Mum wasn't wrong when she claimed I paid as much attention to my hair as I did, for example, to a mani-pedi. In other words, none at all. I'll apply my own nail polish, however sloppily, thanks very much.

I tuned out Mum's passionate insistence that with the right lighting, makeup—and a minor miracle—I could look like a young Charlize Theron. Closing my eyes so no one would witness me rolling them, I shamelessly eavesdropped on the salon's third customer: Edith Newbury, who'd come to visit her sister, Mary Hopkins, and decided to move here. As a Cape Discovery newbie, the mid-seventies widow wasn't yet up to speed with who's who in town. So Angie, who owned Hair Today, was more than happy to fill her in.

Angie: I've done his aunt's hair for years. *Throaty*

chuckle. She's a strange one at times, I have to say, but a real sweetheart all the same.

Edith: Oh, but we're all strange in our own special way, aren't we?

I knew there was a reason I liked Edith almost as much as I did her sister.

Angie: True, true. It's just such a horrific thing to happen in Discovery.

Edith: Awful. I can't imagine the shock of losing a family member that way. And you were saying she's got no one else?

Angie: That's right. He was all she had, so she's on her own now, poor love. *Derogative snort.* Not that he was much of a prize, mind you. I don't know how Birdie put up with him, not after Samuel died. Dominic was her husband's blood, not hers.

Edith: He can't be that bad if he stayed to help his aunt when his uncle passed away, can he?

Angie: *Another snort.* He told anyone who'd listen that he'd left a promising advertising career in Australia, but I reckon the only reason he came over was that he'd nowhere else to go. He probably stuck it out on the farm, hoping he'd inherit everything once Birdie shuffled off.

Edith: Dear me. He sounds like a right swine.

Angie: Oh, he was. Though he became his uncle's right-hand man and did all the heavy lifting around the orchard when Samuel couldn't any longer.

Edith: And after his uncle died?

Angie: *Deep sigh.* He moved into the big house with Birdie, supposedly to keep an eye on her. But without Samuel's knowledge and experience, the orchard stopped doing so well. Money became tight. For Birdie, anyhow. No more luxuries like her regular wash and set appointment.

Long pause. Money problems didn't seem to keep Dominic from boozing down the pub most weekends, of course. It's tragic what's happened to her. Like I said, she's such a sweetheart.

Edith: Maybe I should invite her to join the book club I'm starting up.

Angie: Oh, I'm sure she'd love that. Especially now she has more freedom to get out and about.

Edith: What stopped her before?

Skye finished rubbing a towel over my hair and tapped my shoulder to signal I should sit up. I did—and caught the salon owner's expression. Angie looked as though she'd bitten into a gooey-centered muffin and encountered mustard rather than the anticipated caramel.

"Dominic would be my best guess." She reached for the blow-dryer. Glancing around, she must have noticed she had an audience, so instead of turning it on, she cocked her hip and rested the dryer against it.

"You wanna know what sort of man ends up on the wrong end of a gun? Three weeks ago, Birdie came in for the first time in almost a year. She seemed a little antsy, but I didn't know why." Angie's mouth twisted into a scowl. "I was just about to dry her off when he shows up and starts in on her. 'Why did you lie and tell me you were going to the grocery store?' And 'Why are you wasting money on trying to make yourself look younger?' Poor Birdie insisted on leaving with him then and there, and she paid in cash—lots of coins and five- and ten-dollar notes, like she'd been squirreling them away."

"What a piece of work," my mother said.

"Ugh. Guys like that are such control freaks." Skye gestured to the empty styling chair next to Edith's. Sensibly, well away from my mother, who the salon junior had led to the basin to wait for Angie to finish up. "Went on a date with one once. Guy started off with passive-aggressive suggestions about how I wore my hair. Never made it past that first date."

The conversation then switched to 'Who's Had the Worst First Date?' stories. While my mother jumped into the discussion, Skye quietly asked me what kind of cut I wanted. I told her, and she got to work.

Twenty-five minutes later, I sported an asymmetrical bob that even an amateur such as me could style at home with minimal product and a hairdryer. I loved it. Mum cringed at the sight. So win-win in my book! At least it gave her something else to worry about other than my undate-able-ness. First or otherwise.

Taking advantage of Angie pasting smelly dye on my mother's hair and wrapping strands in foil, I kissed Mum's cheek, thanked her for treating me to a new 'do,' and fled the salon before she could order Skye to 'tidy up my daughter's lopsided hair.'

On reaching the relative safety of the sidewalk, I hooked my phone from my shoulder bag and assumed the selfie position. Well, fumbled with the angle of my phone in order to get a flattering pose and non-extreme close-up while factoring in my lack of coordination when it came to posing and tapping the screen at the same time. When I'd finally lined up everything perfectly, I held it steady and...spotted a cute fluffy dog and the guy walking him behind me. Who was neither fluffy nor cute.

Okay, half that statement's a lie. I'll leave you to guess which half.

My finger jerked reflexively, taking the shot. I spun around. "Hi, Oliver."

Confession: I gave my freshly spruced up curls a nonchalant little flip as I turned, Flirty-McFlirtface style.

Oliver gave a bemused eyebrow raise, perhaps puzzling over whether I was swatting at a bug trapped in my hair. Sadly, it wouldn't be the first time he'd caught me freeing an insect from my curls.

"Hey." His long-legged walk slowed, then stopped in front of me.

Maki, the white Japanese Spitz fuzzball Oliver sweetly exercised for his elderly and infirm neighbor, proceeded to sniff the heck out of my leggings. No doubt the pup caught a whiff of eau de feline on my legs in the form of black kitty hairs.

Oliver cocked his head and examined me from the neck up. My skin warmed both above and below the neckline of my old 'doesn't matter if it gets hair clippings all over it' T-shirt.

"Did you escape Hair Today before the stylist could finish up?" He reached out and gave the longer side of my curls a gentle tug. "Skye, was it?"

Scalp prickling with delicious sensation, I gulped, struggling to arrange my molten-hot features into some semblance of cool composure. It didn't help matters that a nettle of jealousy that Oliver knew the attractive young stylist's name stung my pride. And made me wonder if my attempt at recreating a youthful and hip look had FAIL stamped all over it.

Crinkles appeared around his greeny-blue eyes. "I'm teasing, Tess. I like the new cut; it suits you."

"Thanks." Still smarting a little—and annoyed at myself for allowing other people's opinions to influence my thoughts about how I wore my hair—I leaned away to drop my phone back into my bag.

His hand left my hair and slid into the hip pocket of his jeans. Two beats of awkwardness passed as I made a production of zipping up my shoulder bag, all the while keeping my gaze averted.

"I was just going to grab a to-go coffee from Rosie's and walk this guy along the waterfront," he said. "Wanna join me?"

Coffee and a stroll with Maki, as opposed to a romantic pet-free dinner with an over-eighteen beverage…? Could the guy make it any clearer that he'd slotted me into the friend-zone column of his life?

"Sorry, I have plans. Maybe some other time." Said in the same kiss-off tone one used when promising *I'll call you tomorrow*.

"Oh. Sure."

Given that I'd only recently changed his contact name on my phone from 'Stone's Throw Stud' to boring 'Oliver Novak,' the disturbingly handsome bar owner was no doubt unused to rejection. And given my history with a long-term boyfriend who'd cheated, I wasn't. And I was in no hurry to become intimately acquainted with it again.

Offering him the smile I use on customers who expect me to drop whatever I'm doing to cater to their every whim, I moved to step around him. Nothing wrong with his reflexes—he sidestepped to block me. Unfortunately for him, Maki had finished sniffing my pants and impatiently circled Oliver's legs, the dog's leash looping around his walking buddy's kneecaps. He stumbled, cursing under his breath.

Made a pleasant change from me being the clumsy dolt in any given scenario.

I folded in my lips to prevent a smirk as he untangled himself, Maki bouncing on his front paws in excitement.

During my second attempt to brush past, Oliver touched my arm. "Are you free this afternoon instead? Could I pick you up around three?"

I gazed into gorgeous greeny-blue eyes and went weak-kneed and gooey-centered.

Rookie mistake, Tess. But you've got this. Don't focus on how he smells like finely aged leather despite wearing a fleece-lined denim jacket or the flecks of auburn in his facial stubble that the autumn sun turns to gold. Turn him down. Right now.

"Okay," I squeaked, my vocal cords and willpower having both melted under the dazzle of his smile.

Maki yipped impatiently while yanking on his leash, and with a wave, Oliver continued along the street toward the waterfront. Catching movement in the salon window out of the corner of my eye, I turned to see Skye, Angie, and my mother lined up along the glass. Grinning, waving, and giving me thumbs-up signals. Of course they'd witnessed the whole thing.

Rookie mistake, Tess. Rookie mistake.

SIX

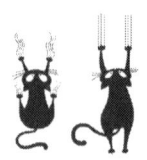

Picture, if you will, the most romantic first date you can imagine.

An intimate candlelight dinner? A stroll along a sunset beach? A surprise trip to Paris on a private plane to dine on caviar at Les Deux Magots?

Okay, that last option would require a much larger time commitment than your average date. Plus a billionaire tycoon or heir to the throne of a largish country. Both options put any men I knew out of the running.

Now picture the weirdest first date you can imagine. Not the worst or the most embarrassing. Nor the one that almost made you give up on dating humans and opt for furry companionship instead. Just the weirdest. Go on, I'll wait…

Got something in mind? Well, let me tell you, your weird wouldn't come close to the weird I was currently enduring on my first 'date' with Oliver Novak.

For starters, there was his mysterious text just after lunch, asking me to bring Kit along in his walking harness. Which he was still getting used to. *Okaaay*. A romantic stroll it was then. With a chubby black cat in tow. I mentally shrugged; who was I to question his choice of furry chaperone?

After selecting indigo-colored jeans, a casual-but-chic sweater, chunky-heeled ankle boots, and a merino-possum blend beret in a buttery yellow that made the whole ensemble pop, I gave Kit a stern lecture about what constituted a good wingman—or wingcat in this instance. Kit responded with a hind paw pointing skyward and a thorough licking of his nether regions. Clearly, I didn't possess Birdie's cat-whispering abilities.

Pearl watched haughtily from high on a neighbor's wall as we waited on the sidewalk for Oliver. He'd texted to say he was on his way, and I'd opted to wait outside, thereby sparing him Harry's twenty-plus questions. None of which would pertain to Oliver's intentions toward his granddaughter—who he said was a strong, independent woman that knew her own worth and would demand respect from any man lucky enough to date her. Or words to that effect.

Harry's actual words had been: "I know the best places around here to bury a body where it'll never be found. He doesn't treat you right, tell me. I'll draw a map for you, girlie."

The throaty growl of an engine rumbled up Cape Street before a black whale of a car lumbered around the corner. Oliver sat behind the wheel—a wheel that was on the wrong side of the vehicle for our roads—and riding shotgun, his head stuck out the window and tongue lolling in the breeze, Maki. Gearheads might have dreamed about this behemoth, in the USA and *waaay* back in the sixties, but here in new-millennium New Zealand, it was as out of time and place as The Beatles.

And it was love at first sight.

Best. Pickup-for-a-date. Ever!

"Hop in," he said.

Clad in a long-sleeved polo shirt shoved up to the elbow, a stylized logo embroidered on its shoulder, Oliver rested his forearm on the sill of the lowered driver's window. He twisted in his cherry-red leather seat, turning to the dog to order him into the back.

Maki, however, chose to ignore him and continued to pant and drool out the passenger window as I walked around the car. Spotting Kit in my arms appeared to refocus his attention, and he gave an excited yip. Eager to touch noses with his new canine best buddy, Kit strained forward with a greeting, *"Purrrpt?"*

Yes, unlike his sister, Kit had decided this particular dog was friend not foe. I suspected Kit's actual motivation in befriending Maki was to have the canine version of a bodyguard on his side should he choose to assert his dominance within the neighborhood cats' territory.

Finally relenting, Maki squeezed through the gap to sit on the back bench seat, so I climbed in and settled Kit onto my lap.

"Nice Dodge," I said, pretending I knew a Dodge from a Daihatsu. I totally didn't. But the white embroidered D.O.D.G.E below the logo stood in stark contrast to the navy knit fabric of Oliver's shirt.

"Thanks." A crescent of teeth flashed in my direction. Score one for the armchair detective, baby. "It's a nineteen sixty-four *blah, blah, blah* with a *blah, blah, blah*."

Yeah. I tuned out the enthusiastic car-trivia details Oliver provided as we pulled away from the curb. Watching his lips form words and the way his shirt stretched in all the right places as he worked the stick shift through the gears was far more fascinating. Don't get me wrong; I loved the car. In a 'that's a cool car, take me for a ride in it' kind of way rather than a 'tell me the make, model, and history since it rolled off the showroom floor.'

But even with all the car talk, the occasional tongue swipe across my nape courtesy of the pooch behind me, and a kitty who thought sitting on my lap in the front seat was akin to being trapped in an escape room, it was still, so far, the best date I'd been on in years.

Until, instead of heading out of town for the picnic I'd begun to envisage, Oliver drove the Dodge into a parking lot. A parking lot belonging to Sunnyville Nursing Home.

Say what now?

I turned to my chauffeur—and I use that term with a twist of sarcasm since I'd neither asked nor expected our date to take place in front of the small crowd of elderly residents staring at us from the nursing home's windows—with my politest smile. "Are we picking someone up on the way?"

Like, perhaps his grandparents, who'd accompany the two of us—four, including our furry hitchhikers—on an afternoon cruise? Which would be a little odd. But sweet.

I guess.

"Nope. There's no 'on the way.' We've arrived," he said.

We had? *This* was the destination he'd chosen for our first date? I guess my bewilderment must have shown on my face.

"Maki and I visit once a month," Oliver explained while unclipping his seat belt. "He gets cuddles and treats from the residents, then I give some of the oldies a ride in the Dodge. Brightens the residents' day, and I figure if they love Maki, they'll love petting Kit too."

A 'V' appearing between his eyebrows, his voice trailed

as he registered my not-so-convincing poker face. "*Oh*. Did you think that I...damn, I mean, that *we* were...?"

"*Pfft*, of course not." I attacked my seat belt one-handed, as Kit seemed desperate to join Maki and apparently wanted to use my beret as a launching pad to do so. "It's a nice idea. Very nice—*very great*—actually. And bonus, I get to check off a good deed done for the day."

About the same time my tongue grew tired of flapping, I managed to release my seat belt. And the universe must've been in a generous mood because with Kit's belly covering my face, Oliver couldn't see the prickle of mortified tears in my eyes.

"Tessa. I'm sor—"

"If we hurry," I blurted in the hope of drowning out his apology, my lips tickling against Kit's soft fur, "we'll score some afternoon tea. Beth reckons they do a mean scone with jam and whipped cream here."

I scrambled out of the car as fast as one can with a plus-size cat clinging to one's face *Alien* style and while fighting a door as cumbersome as a bank vault's. Most likely resembling a jack-in-the-box, I popped out of the whale's belly and bent to peel the grumbling feline off my head. Craftily avoiding Oliver's eyes and any embarrassed pity contained therein.

He must've gotten the hint that I had no interest in discussing this unmitigated disaster of a non-date any further, as he collected Maki from the back seat and attached his hot-pink leash in silence. We walked into Sunnyville and were greeted by a smiling nurse, who led us through to the airy lounge. Saved from further awkwardness by the sheer number of excited residents, I headed for one of my granddad's longtime friends and plonked Kit on his lap.

While Maki did the rounds like an old pro, I couldn't help but admire the easy way Oliver had with the residents who wanted to pet the white fluffball. He seemed genuinely interested in what they had to say, listening more than he contributed to their conversations—a skill sadly lacking in many of the men I'd dated in the past.

Not that Oliver and I were on a date, and it sure didn't require a sleuth's magnifying glass to read the writing on this wall. The flirty moment we'd shared in February was just that—a moment. Back then, he'd been the one embarrassed and put on the spot, almost coerced by my friends and family to officially ask me out. Guess we were even now.

I ducked my head, letting my wonky hair—as Sean teasingly called it this morning—shield my face while Oliver and Maki passed by. Needn't have bothered. After handing the pup to one of the staff, Oliver left with his entourage of car buffs, all loudly discussing horsepower and torque. As Kit had settled himself into a purring loaf shape on the seat next to a lady who insisted on calling him Bubba, I put her in charge of his kitty leash while I fetched us both a fresh cup of tea.

When I returned five minutes later, I was met with the sight of a staff member holding a growling Kit aloft, à la Lion King. Whipped cream covered Kit's face while he clenched the evidence of his thievery in his mouth, his front paws wrapped protectively around a mangled scone.

THE STAFF MEMBER, none other than Gavin Schmidt, turned to me with a chuckle. "Your four-legged predator, I presume?"

Muttering apologies, I set down the two cups on an end table. Honestly, I didn't quite know what to do next. The scone was beyond saving, and besides, if I attempted to reclaim it, there'd be crumbs and jam and whipped cream spread in a blast pattern over Sunnyville's lounge.

"Why don't we go through to the kitchen to take it off him and clean him up?" Gavin twisted Kit around as if requesting his permission.

Kit's ears flattened and the growling resumed. In his feline opinion, he'd hunted the scone fair and square, and no one was stealing it away.

Gah! I was starting to sound like Birdie.

Speaking of Birdie... I couldn't resist an opportunity to flex my curiosity.

"Yes please," I said. "And I'm so sorry about your scone," I said to the woman he'd stolen it from—who was now stroking a lumbar cushion while telling it what a naughty kitty it was.

I followed Gavin and the scone crumbs out of the lounge, palming them as I went like some grown-up Hansel and Gretel hot on the trail of home. And oh, how I wanted to just flee homeward and bury my troubles in a tub of hokey pokey ice cream.

As the double doors to the industrial kitchen hissed shut behind us, Gavin led me over to the corner where they rinsed and stacked the plates into massive dishwashers.

"Spray rinser?" He angled his head toward the hose-nozzle combo sitting over the sink.

"I'd suggest not if you want to keep the skin on your arms intact." I stared meaningfully at his short-sleeved yellow shirt. "Just set him down on the floor."

He did, and Kit assumed the hunched *this is mine, back off* stance.

"You gonna let him eat it?" Gavin asked with a heavy note of chastisement in his tone.

I crouched beside Kit, who couldn't seem to decide whether to release the chunk in his mouth and gulp it down before a human could intervene or hold on to it until he could dash to a safe place where he couldn't be reached. Not gonna happen with my hand now securely wrapped around his harness. "Nope. We don't reward criminal behavior. Do we, big guy?"

Gavin grunted. "Tell that to Marcus and everyone else who wants to ruin Discovery."

Precisely the lead-in I'd hoped for. "Was that what you and your group were protesting about yesterday?"

"Hall acts like he'd be doing the town a favor if Pavlova Productions chose his property to film on. He can only see it through a lens of greed and what he can make on the deal."

Before Gavin saw this as a conversion opportunity and gave me the full environmental spiel, I held up a hand. "Marcus's land wasn't their first choice according to gossip, was it?"

He frowned. "No. The MacKenzies definitely had the advantage there, even though their block is smaller. Hall's cleared much of the native bush off his property for his massive orchards—and don't get me started on the damage that's done—so that took it out of the running. Initially."

Risking the wrath of Kit, I pulled the scone remains from his mouth and tossed them into a nearby trashcan. "But Birdie wouldn't allow Pavlova to bulldoze her cattery no matter how much they offered in return." I tilted my head back from my lowered position so I could study his expression. "You must've been happy about that…until Dominic made it known he supported the whole three-ring circus coming to town, along with the money they'd bring."

"Dominic would never have changed his aunt's mind." Gavin pulled a *whatever* face. "So, if you can't convince 'em, ship 'em off to an old folks' home and do whatever the heck you like."

My stomach flip-flopped, tossing the one-and-a-half scones I'd eaten over in an ungainly lurch. *"What?"*

"Oh, yeah. Mrs. MacKenzie and her nephew came for a tour of Sunnyville a few weeks before Easter." He gave a sour chuckle. "Though Mrs. MacKenzie had no idea she was here to pick out a room. Dominic must've told her she was here for a special lunch because she kept asking what time the party started."

"You were working that day?"

"Yep. And there was nothing special scheduled that day —a Friday, I remember, because we had our usual fish 'n' chip lunch. We encourage the elderly out in the community to come in for a meal, though. It's cheap for them and good for the oldies to see new faces." His expression brightened. "You should bring your granddad up for the Sunday roast tomorrow. Afterward, Mrs. Salmon from Saint Barnabas plays the piano, and the residents have a bit of a sing-along."

"I'll mention it to him," I said, straightening.

Harry would sooner eat roast roadkill and sing along to a death metal soundtrack than spend his Sunday afternoon in Sunnyville. "But back to the MacKenzies. How did Birdie react when she found she wasn't here for a party?"

"She was upset." Gavin clicked his tongue in sympathy. "Can't say I blame her. The patronizing way Dominic spoke to her: like she was a not-too-bright five-year-old. 'Look how pretty the garden is, Auntie,'" he mimicked Dominic's voice. "'They have bingo every Wednesday afternoon—you'd like that, wouldn't you?'"

"Did you give the MacKenzies their tour?" I asked.

He shook his head. "No, the manager's in charge of that. But I overheard Dominic telling Melissa that his aunt was senile and stubborn as a mule about her independence, so the idea of her moving here needed to be handled delicately."

I blew out my lips in a disgusted snort. "Birdie isn't senile. She's a little..." *Quirky? Eccentric?* "alternative in the way she looks at the world, but she appears to have every one of her marbles accounted for and in the right place."

"I agree," Gavin said. "Nothing I saw made me think she needed to leave her home and move into full-time care."

Glancing down at Kit, I swallowed a sigh. He was now happily focused on swiping the dregs of whipped cream off his face with his paw. "Tell me what happened when Birdie found out why she was really here."

Gavin leaned against the counter, settling into his story. "Well, I was helping Mr. Peters back to his room when Melissa passed us, hurrying down the hallway to her office. The MacKenzies were standing outside one of our empty rooms, and neither of them noticed us. Dominic did a complete Jekyll and Hyde, switching from patronizing to outright aggressive, his voice getting louder and louder. Crazy old bat, he called her." Gavin's expression darkened into a fierce scowl. "He told her she was moving in at the end of the month, one way or another. I couldn't hear her reply because Mr. Peters insisted he needed the bathroom at that point, but I noticed her dab her eyes with a hankie."

My blood pressure rocketed into the stratosphere. "What a low-down, cowardly, bullying...gah!" I was so furious that I couldn't think of an insult harsh enough.

"My thoughts exactly. My mum always said you can tell a lot about a man by the way he treats animals...and those close to him. Anyway, I'd better get back to work." Gavin pushed away from the counter, ducked to scratch Kit behind his ears, then moved past me toward the kitchen door.

He pushed it open and looked back at me with an inscrutable hint of a smile. "Could understand why Birdie might want to find someone to take care of her problem, you know?"

And then he was gone.

Leaving me to wonder—with a growing sense of unease—had Birdie fixed her problem nephew via a murder-for-hire solution?

SEVEN

I took the low-down, cowardly option of calling my brother for a ride, invoking the 'don't ask questions; don't tell Mum' sibling clause. I'd waited until Oliver's Dodge prowled out of the lot to take three grinning residents for a quick blast around the coast, then rang Sean. And when he pulled into Sunnyville's parking lot, I'd slunk into his car with Kit in my arms. On our short drive home, I sent Oliver a text message to apologize for leaving Sunnyville early, explaining that Kit had developed an upset stomach.

Which was kind of the truth. There was an upset stomach in the equation, just not the one belonging to the smug feline purring on my lap.

Almost made it home without my little brother poking his nose into my business too. However, as he parked right outside Unraveled, he opened his mouth. "Mum said you and Oliver were—"

"Uh!" I barked, cutting him off and pointing a threatening finger at his nose. "Not one more word."

"But—"

"No buts. I have, over the course of the past thirty-two

years, created an internal spreadsheet of all the things you've done, said, and lied about to our parents. Do you really want to unleash me, the keeper of all secrets, upon your world?"

He held up both palms with a grin and then made a zipping motion across his lips. "Enjoy the rest of your afternoon, Sis."

I would've enjoyed the rest of my afternoon too—because every time Oliver's face popped up in my brain, I managed to push it down into the primordial swamp of *Stuff to Deal with Later*—but I couldn't stop thinking about Gavin's parting words. At half-past four, I admitted defeat, whipped up a casserole dish of cottage pie, and drove out to Birdie's.

She cracked open the door at my knock. "Oh, Tessa. I wasn't expecting you."

Darn. I'd forgotten to let her know I was bringing her a meal in all my rushing around. "Sorry. I've brought you dinner." I held the foil-covered dish aloft with oven-mitted hands.

Immediately brightening, she flung the door wide—except she'd forgotten to remove the security chain, so it shuddered before slamming shut. After a series of rattles, Birdie opened the door again with a sheepish smile. "April insists I keep the chain on when she's not here."

"Sounds a sensible idea." I followed her into the kitchen and placed the cottage pie on the counter.

While peeling off the oven mitts, I glanced around the room, which appeared to have been scrubbed from top to bottom. Every surface that was meant to shine shone. Every countertop had been emptied of clutter, and the mishmash of envelopes, junk mail, and what had looked like a library of cookbooks that I'd peripherally noticed on Thursday evening, all gone. A peek into the living room revealed carpet so clean you could've eaten off it—were you that way inclined—and the distinct absence of Dominic's Throne. In its place stood a plush-looking sofa with a couple of crocheted knee rugs artfully tossed across it.

"Wow. You've been spring-cleaning?"

Birdie chuckled. "Oh, no. It's all April. Up before me this morning—cleaning, cleaning, cleaning. She's gone through every room in the house and given it a real spruce up. Plus, she's helped me with the animals and made sure I eat three square meals every day. She's been such a godsend. I shooed her off to the pub tonight to have a drink with her friends."

I gave her arm a reassuring rub. "Can I borrow her when you're done? Please?"

"She'll make a lovely wife for some lucky man one day," Birdie said. "And not just because she's a domestic goddess." She scooped up Cheddar, who'd been weaving around our ankles, and buried her nose in the soft fur right behind his ear—my favorite spot to snuffle too. "Once she stops being so self-conscious about her teeth and plays up her other assets. Like her kind and generous nature."

"Those traits can so easily be overlooked. It's certainly sweet of April to take such good care of you while she's here." Although the thought of her walking around the MacKenzie property by herself on Friday afternoon still irrationally bugged me.

"I very much appreciate it." Birdie shot me a sidelong glance filled with trepidation. "But I wondered if I could impose on you to drive me to the meeting with the funeral director on Monday morning. I'd feel more comfortable with someone I know a little better."

"It's no imposition whatsoever. I'd be happy to be your

driver and provide whatever support I can during the meeting."

Beaming at me, she kissed Cheddar's head—which was now straining in the direction of the warm-meaty-smelling casserole dish—and set him down. "Thank you. But, oh my word, I wasn't thinking—you don't have to stay at Morrigans with me if it brings up sad memories of your nana."

"According to Harry, Stewart Morrigan and his staff looked after Nana Dee-Dee brilliantly, so I'm sure they'll look after Dominic too."

Birdie's gaze shifted from my face to study something beyond my shoulder. Now seemed as good a time as any to segue into the topic of her tumultuous relationship with her nephew.

"Stewart will give him the same respect Dominic gave you." I kept my voice neutral as I leaned a hip against the counter, watching the tendons in Birdie's throat tighten as her jaw clenched. "And he treated you well, didn't he? Moving into the house after Samuel died, keeping the orchard going and helping you with the animals."

"Yes, he did," she forced through stiff lips. "He was a lovely little boy...and a good man."

"But he wasn't so good to you lately, was he, Birdie?"

When she remained silent, I continued, "I was at Sunnyville this afternoon, and one of the staff told me he'd seen you and Dominic there a few weeks ago...fighting."

Her eyes flicked to mine. "We weren't *fighting*. It was just a difference of opinion, is all."

"He wanted to put you into the nursing home, and you didn't want to go," I said. "That sounds like a *big* difference of opinion. And you were upset at him for tricking you into visiting Sunnyville, weren't you?"

"Yes, I was." Mouth puckering into a furious bud, she

slapped a palm on the countertop. Claws scrabbling on the floor, Cheddar took off out of the kitchen at a run. "He had no right to try to force me to leave my home—*my* home, not his—and into that place with a bunch of old people. I'm not senile or gaga like he told everyone, but I would be after a week living in Sunnyville."

As a terrible, black-as-death shadow rose to the surface of my mind, I moistened suddenly dry lips and took a deep, cleansing breath. "Birdie," I said as calmly as I could, given my doubts, "is there anything about your nephew's death that you want to get off your chest?"

Her wide-eyed gaze filled with tears, and she pressed her fingers to her lips, hiccupping back a sob. Then her spine stiffened as if she were gathering courage.

"Yes, Tessa, I do. It was me. I killed him."

GEE WHISKERS! Of all the things Birdie could've confessed, offing her nephew wasn't one I'd anticipated. My jaw metaphorically hit the floor. "You did what now?"

She extended her wrists toward me. They trembled. "Put me under citizen's arrest, honeybunch. I deserve it."

I gently grasped her wrists and turned them until I clasped her hands. "Rubbish. Now, tell me exactly what you mean. How could you have killed your nephew when you were with me at Unraveled all evening?"

And Dominic had been alive and obnoxious when I'd collected Birdie on Thursday evening. He'd hollered from somewhere inside the house, telling his aunt not to spend all her money on 'more wool and crap.' Charm personified.

Birdie hung her head. "I slipped pills into his beer before I left."

Ah. So that explained her beer bottle rinsing and recycling frenzy after I'd discovered her nephew's body. Hated to even think it, but that hadn't been the act of a slightly gaga old lady. That had been planned, premeditated...*something*. I couldn't bring myself to think the 'm' word, so I swallowed it. "What sort of pills?"

"Sleeping pills. I had some left from when Samuel passed away. I needed them in the first few weeks."

My eyebrows scrunched together. "Are you sure they were sleeping pills, Birdie?"

If they were, Dominic should've been flaked out on his throne when we arrived home, not lying in the laundry room on the other side of the house.

"Almost certain they were." She tugged on my hand. "Come, I'll show you."

I allowed her to lead me out of the kitchen and down the hallway to her bedroom. Photographs of Birdie and Samuel blanketed one wall of faded rose bouquet wallpaper, with another dedicated entirely to animals—cats, dogs, hedgehogs, birds, guinea pigs, lambs, alpacas, calves. My guess, every animal Birdie had ever cared for.

Perched on the edge of the bed, she slid open the nightstand drawer and rummaged around, setting pills rattling in what sounded like multiple plastic containers. "Which one was it? The blue lid? Yes, yes. Or maybe white? No—definitely blue." Birdie pulled out two thumb-sized bottles.

Both had blue lids and pharmacy-printed labels on their sides. Holding both bottles close to her nose, then out a short distance, she squinted at the tiny print. After shaking both containers with a quizzical expression, she seemed to come to a decision. "This one," she announced, offering me one of the small bottles. "There's only a couple of pills left in it now."

My fingers closed around the cool plastic, but Birdie didn't release it. She leaned toward me. "I don't think I intended to kill him, at least, not consciously. I just wanted him to sleep for a bit and not badger me when I got home. You do believe me, don't you?"

Sitting there with her slumped shoulders and hangdog expression, she looked so frail. The animal photos stared accusingly down at me from the wall. Birdie harm a living creature? *Preposterous*, they all seemed to mew-bark-tweet-baa-moo.

"Of course." Taking a seat next to her on the bed, I pasted on a smile that didn't quite fit and plucked the bottle from her fingers. I held it at optimum reading distance.

Bridget MacKenzie. For constipation, take one tablet daily with food.

I reread the printed label. Twice. The bottle was opaque, so I cracked it open and peered at the remaining contents. "You're positive these are the pills you spiked Dominic's beer with?"

"Absolutely."

"And how many did you use?"

"Only three. One for each beer." She gave a small shrug. "I used to take one pill to help me sleep, so I figured with Dominic being so much bigger, he'd need at least double the dose and one more for luck."

Luck? I wasn't sure luck had anything to do with the result of taking three of these pills in rapid succession. No wonder Dominic had been rushing to his bathroom!

I screwed the lid on the bottle and returned it. "Birdie, these are laxatives, not sleeping pills."

"They are?" She squinted at the label again. "Well, I'll be."

Birdie dropped both pill bottles back into her nightstand drawer and slid me the side-eye. "Are you going to turn me in to the coppers?"

"For, er, unclogging your nephew's plumbing?"

"No. For tampering with evidence at a crime scene. I rinsed out Dominic's beer bottles."

Apparently, she *had* been paying close attention to Gary Sinise and his CSI team.

"You didn't know it was a crime scene at the time," I said.

Had she though? No. Of course not. Birdie couldn't possibly have shot her nephew; therefore, an unknown suspect must be responsible. Or an unsub. Birdie and Harry weren't the only ones who watched too many crime shows on TV.

"I figured Dominic must've taken himself to bed to sleep it off, and it's a habit I've gotten into—tidying up after him. Making a rod for my own back, as Samuel used to say."

Sounded plausible, and I truly wanted to believe her. Besides, if Dominic had anything other than laxatives in his system, I'd bet on Detective Mana's team finding it.

"If I hadn't doctored Dom's beer, he'd have been snoring in the living room when the burglar broke into the house. Then he'd still be alive." Birdie shuddered, wrapping her arms around her waist.

Maybe. Maybe her nephew had surprised a thief and been shot. But what sort of thief took only electronic devices and didn't bother searching the house for other valuables? Not a very competent one, in my opinion.

"I'm wondering if theft was the intruder's real motive," I said. "This is small-town New Zealand. Taking a gun along on a burglary is like swatting a fly with a baseball bat. It's overkill, and you're more likely to hurt yourself than the fly."

Birdie's eyes widened. "You think someone broke into the house to kill Dominic? *Deliberately?*" She unwrapped a hand from her waist and pressed it to her mouth. "Oh my word. Who would do such a thing?"

"Can you think of anyone who would want him...out of the picture?"

"You mean dead? Why would anyone want him dead? I know he wasn't the easiest man to be around—Lord knows he could be horrid with a few drinks under his belt. But it wasn't like he had a pirate's treasure hidden under the floorboards in his room—Dom only seemed to have enough spare cash for his Saturday nights at the pub, never enough to pop down to Hanburys for bread and milk. He had no assets other than his truck, which he was still paying off, no life insurance, and no dependents who could claim it even if he did..." She shook her head. "It makes no sense. Unless..." Her head tilted to one side, frown lines furrowing her brow. "Marcus Hall. Of course!"

Tingles raced across my scalp and down my neck at the way she'd said her neighbor's name. "What about Marcus?"

"That snake's always had his eye on our land, and with Dominic gone, he's one step closer to getting his greedy hands on it."

Before I could form a response, the sound of tires crunching over gravel reached my ears. April home from the pub already? I shadowed Birdie as she made her way through the house to the front door. Ridiculous perhaps, but I worried the intruder might return to finish what he—or she—started.

"That's not April's car. Who could it be?" Birdie muttered as we stepped outside. "I'm not expecting company."

A woman who looked to be in her mid-twenties

emerged from a Volkswagen Beetle convertible. Wavy hair the shade of good espresso spilled down the back of her plain-but-elegant black dress, and as she turned to shut the car door, her slender body moved with all the grace of a prima ballerina. *If* said ballerina had half a watermelon stuffed up her dress: Birdie's visitor was pregnant.

The woman turned toward us, a small smile curving a mouth set among bold but feminine features. Full lips, olive complexion, a slightly hooked nose—and as she drew closer, melted-chocolate-colored eyes that men must imagine drowning in.

"Hello, Mrs. MacKenzie," she said in a voice as smooth as her chocolatey eyes. She stopped at the foot of the step leading onto the verandah. "I must apologize in advance for dropping in on you at such a sad time. I'm Cora Rossi." The younger woman's introduction carried weight; she announced herself as if expecting some sort of recognition from Birdie.

When I darted a sideways glance to gauge whether my friend knew this unexpected guest, those tingles returned in earnest.

Birdie looked as though a ghost had just materialized in front of us.

EIGHT

"Y-you..." Birdie's voice quavered, and I swear she started to sway. Instinctively, I hooked an arm through hers, just in case. "You look just like him."

Who?

However, I didn't get a chance to voice my question because the woman—Cora—spoke again. "My mother always said so. God rest her soul." She crossed herself, her smile transforming into a suitably solemn expression. "I'm Samuel MacKenzie's granddaughter."

She was who? Birdie and Samuel never had children. And as far as I knew, they'd been high school sweethearts and married young.

Cora hurried up the step and attached herself to Birdie's other arm. "I've given you a terrible shock, haven't I? I'm so sorry."

"It's all right," Birdie said. "But I think we'd all better go inside and have a cup of tea, or maybe a sip of something stronger." She blinked down at the younger woman's rounded belly, now nudging against her side. "Not you, though."

"No, not me." Cora patted her baby bump. "I'll stick to tea thanks—herbal if you have it."

"I've got some peppermint tea bags in the pantry."

"Delightful."

Birdie's arm flexed against mine as she turned toward Cora. "Oh"—she swung back to me—"this is my friend Tessa. She's thoughtfully brought me a lovely casserole for dinner."

Substantially taller than Birdie, Cora sent me a dazzling smile over the top of her head. "Ah, is that the mouth-wateringly delicious smell?"

"I guess so." For some inexplicable reason, Miss Rossi had thrown me off my game. As a former high school guidance counselor, I prided myself in my ability to sense when people were hiding something—*No, Miss Wakefield, it wasn't me that drank the bottle of red wine my mum uses for cooking*—but I couldn't get a read on her.

However, I'd give her the benefit of the doubt. For now.

"We'll have a cuppa, and you can tell me all about yourself, and maybe afterward, you'd like to stay for a bite to eat." Birdie unhooked her arm from mine and let Cora usher her inside.

I traipsed after them because, call me Suspicious Sally, I wasn't prepared to leave Birdie alone with a stranger. Even if that stranger was female and pregnant. In my limited experience, women could be just as dangerous as men.

In the kitchen, Cora sat at the dining table while Birdie switched on the kettle and bustled around fetching tea bags and her *only for company* china cups and saucers. Noted immediately: Cora chose the seat at the head of the table in a subtle but classic power play. She rested her forearm on the tabletop and crossed one long leg over the other. As a counter to her relaxed pose, her dark gaze skimmed the room in what I perceived as an assessing manner. I'd seen the same sort of focus from my realtor mother whenever she entered someone's house for the first time.

Sizing it up. Mentally carrying out a property evaluation.

Then again, perhaps Cora was a fan of kitschy Kiwiana decor, circa nineteen seventies.

Birdie set steaming cups of water with floating tea bags in front of us and took the seat across from mine. After whipping out her tea bag—which I knew from experience she'd reuse at least twice more—she placed it on the saucer and inhaled deeply. As if preparing herself for words that would tear open old wounds. "Please, tell me everything you know."

My heart went out to her. Any time Birdie mentioned her late husband, she'd get this adorable twinkle in her eyes. Almost as though she knew his absence was only temporary. A marital in-joke because, at any moment, she expected him to pop in and surprise her with a handful of wildflowers from the orchard. How could she bear knowing that her beloved Samuel had a child with another woman?

Cora reached over and placed her hand on top of Birdie's. "First off, I'm sorry Grandpa isn't around to tell his side of the story. I so would have loved to meet him."

Birdie gave her a quivery smile. "He was a wonderful man, and I'm sure he would have loved meeting you too. Don't you think, Tessa?"

Two pairs of eyes swung my way. Cora referring to Samuel as 'Grandpa' before Birdie had any concrete proof seemed a bit on the nose—in my humble opinion.

"Sure he would've." And then, straight after that introduction, he'd have ordered a DNA test. Samuel MacKenzie was no fool.

An eyebrow arch from Cora, but her pleasant expression remained in place. I translated the arch to mean she didn't care about my opinion one way or another. One beat later, she'd turned back to Birdie, squeezing her hand to reclaim her full attention. "Your Samuel and my grandmother, Irene, met when he was nineteen and she was seventeen."

Birdie's face scrunched in concentration—I could almost see her doing the math in her head. "Samuel would've been at university. We were high school sweethearts, but we agreed not to be too serious until he got his degree. Or exclusive, as they call it nowadays, I believe."

Cora nodded. "That's right. Well, Irene fell pregnant just before she and her family moved to Invercargill. She didn't realize she was pregnant until she was over halfway along."

"Terribly shameful in those days, being an unwed mother." Birdie tutted.

"Her family thought so. When my mother, Roberta, was born, they told everyone she was a late-in-life baby, and my great-grandmother raised her as her own. My mother thought Irene was her big sister until her twenty-first birthday, when they had a little heart-to-heart."

"Your mother never contacted Samuel?" I asked.

Cora shook her head. "She refused to. Said it was best to let sleeping dogs lie. As I got older, she'd tell me bits and pieces about him that her mum had told her. But I didn't know his last name until after she passed away six weeks ago and I went through her things."

"So Samuel never knew he had a daughter...or granddaughter?" The naked hope in Birdie's voice that her husband hadn't lied to her all those years was apparent, even to me.

"As far as I'm aware. And from what my mum said, he was a good man, an honorable man. Given the opportunity, I believe he would've done the right thing by Granny Irene."

"Oh, I'm sure he would've," Birdie said earnestly. "There's no way he would have abandoned a girl he'd gotten in the family way if he'd known."

"I'm happy to take a DNA test, you know, just to be sure."

"There's no need for that—you're the spit of him, honeybunch."

From stranger to 'honeybunch' in less than half an hour? This Cora Rossi sure didn't muck about.

"You're too sweet." After giving Birdie's hand a final pat, she picked up her teacup and took a delicate sip.

"So, Cora, do you live close to Cape Discovery?" I was almost certain she wasn't a local; a woman that attractive would make my single brother's radar go nuts if she did.

Her cup clinked daintily on its saucer. "The rural lifestyle's a complete mystery to me." She gave a self-deprecating chuckle. "I'm city-girl through and through. I scarcely know one end of a cow from another—but I'd love to see the property you and Samuel created together."

Birdie beamed at her. "I'll give you a guided tour tomorrow morning—oh, speaking of which, where are you staying?"

And perched on the tip of my tongue: when had she arrived in town? Just in time to hear about Dominic's untimely demise?

"The Starfish Motel, I think it's called. It's, ah...nice." Said with a wince and a hand pressed to her lower back.

"Oh my word," Birdie said. "You mustn't spend another night on those dreadful old mattresses. After dinner, you'll pick up your things from the motel and stay in my guest room."

I raised a finger with the silent objection that Birdie knew nothing about this woman other than she claimed to be Samuel's granddaughter, but they failed to notice.

"If you're sure I won't be a bother..." Cora said.

"You're Samuel's family; how could you possibly be a bother?"

And just like that, Birdie accepted Cora Rossi into the MacKenzie fold.

EVERY SUNDAY, at the crack of dawn—or so it seemed to those of us who weren't morning people—the Cape Discovery Primary School hosted a farmers market on its grounds. During fine weather, local produce growers set up their stalls in the school's large parking lot, and if rain should dare to fall on the Sabbath, the stall owners made use of the large assembly hall. And fruit and vegetables weren't the only items on offer, oh no.

There were also stalls selling meat and fish, freshly baked artisan bread, pickles and preserves, and enough other goodies to make the market my favorite place to visit on a Sunday morning.

Yet another reason the vicar of Saint Barnabas wasn't my number one fan. Though I had spotted him and his wife getting handsy with a crate of avocados or peaches more than once.

This Sunday, I went against my natural tendencies and got up early. As in, *early* early, when the sun had barely shown its face above the crescent of the bay. So as not to disturb the cats, I pulled on a sweater and skinny jeans in the dark.

Crocheted market bags dangling from my arm—our own 'Happy Hooker' Mary Hopkins made them in bulk to sell from a market stall of her own—I strode out into the brisk morning air. I'll admit, other than picking up some sun-ripened apples and plums—and eggplants if I could find them because I was dying to trick Harry into eating them in a lasagna—there was a reason for me venturing out at this ungodly hour. The trucks would still be unloading their goods on the school grounds, and with any luck, I'd catch Marcus Hall supervising his army of minions.

Three generations of Marcus's family had worked their acres of land in Cape Discovery, and it was his late father who'd started the farmers market. The Halls remained its primary sponsor—something Marcus liked to remind the locals by driving his produce into town each week. Of course, he never stayed long after chatting with a few of the commoners; the man was far too important to do any actual work.

Sure enough, as I entered the bustling parking lot filling rapidly with huge crates of every imaginable fruit and vegetable, I spotted him leaning against the side of his truck. Half a dozen young men swarmed around him, muscling boxes of the apples Halls' orchard was known for. These weren't the export-quality apples they shipped nationally and internationally, but I had to admit, even their seconds were crisp and delicious.

Just imagine how many more of those valuable apples he could grow if he secured the MacKenzie property.

With that in mind, plus the memory of the man's nasty smirk as he'd walked away from us on Friday morning, I adjusted my trajectory toward him. Clad in his usual salt-of-the-earth attire of flannel shirt and jeans, he continued to swipe his thumb across his phone screen right up until I stopped in front of him and cleared my throat.

"Marcus?"

His gaze rose to meet mine with insolent slowness. "Ah. Hello again, Teresa."

"Tessa," I corrected with a plastic smile.

"Nice to see you again." He dipped his chin toward his staff setting up the portable cash registers. "Tell the boys I said to give you a couple of bags of Hall's finest. On the house."

Grand gesture made, he returned to his scrolling.

"As a matter of fact, I'm here to ask you who might've had a problem with Dominic MacKenzie and also knew their way around your property."

Apparently, I'd hung out with Rosie long enough that her lack of filter had rubbed off on me.

My question certainly got Marcus's attention. His bushy eyebrows arrowing together, he glared at me while shoving his phone in his shirt pocket. The top of the screen remained visible, and I glimpsed the banner of the site he'd been perusing: KiwiConnect.

A New Zealand *dating* site. Well, well. The mind boggles.

Marcus stopped slouching against the truck and straightened to his full height. "Are you accusing me of something, Miss Wakefield?"

Finding myself almost nose to collarbone with the farmer—with only his straining belly between us—I backed up a step and planted hands on hips, attempting to appear unintimidated. Doubtful I was pulling it off because, beer belly aside, Marcus looked strong enough to tear down an apple tree and break it into kindling with his bare hands.

"I'm asking as Birdie's friend, one who's worried about a murderer returning to the scene of the crime."

"And why would they do that?"

"Maybe Dominic wasn't the only target of whoever broke in and shot him."

"Who on earth would want to harm a helpless old biddy like Bridget MacKenzie?" Marcus's lip curled, but it was the flickering movement of his fingers tapping out a staccato rhythm on his thigh that caught my attention.

"Someone who sees the tenth commandment as more of a suggestion." At his blank look, I clarified: "Don't covet thy neighbor's stuff."

As a vein bulged in his neck, his bulbous nose turned a brighter shade of red. "You're meddling in things you know nothing about, girlie." His acid-tipped words dripped from between gritted teeth, but I forced myself to stand my ground.

Never show a bully you're afraid.

And Harry was the only man in the world who could call me 'girlie' without me experiencing an overwhelming urge to kick them straight in the family jewels.

My spine stiffened. "What I understand is that Dominic is dead, and now you have a shot at muscling in on MacKenzie land. Sounds like a classic motive for murder to me."

Marcus's gaze flatlined, and he barked out a humorless laugh. "You believe your own propaganda, because you obviously haven't thought it through." Turkey-like, his double chin jutted forward. "As I said, you know nothing about the dynamics between myself and the MacKenzies. I can't deny that owning their property would be another feather in my cap, but I'm a patient man, and Birdie isn't getting any younger. Why risk prison time when Mother Nature will take care of things for me?"

"Aren't you forgetting that, as her only living relative, Dominic would've inherited it all?"

He folded his arms across his barrel-like chest with a smirk. "Exactly. And Dominic was only too eager to sell that millstone around his neck to the highest bidder. Which, in this case, would be..." He flicked a thumb at himself.

I blinked, my neck jerking backward. "He was? But I thought the orchard meant *something* to him. I've heard he left a promising advertising career in Aussie to work the land with his uncle."

Marcus snorted. "You're delusional if you believe for one second that a greedy little prat like Dominic would leave a promising career. If he left Australia of his own volition, it was for more selfish reasons than helping out family." He shook his head. "Doesn't take a genius to figure out he planned to ship his batty aunt off to Sunnyville, take Pavlova's offer if presented with one, and then sell the land to me. Maximizing his profits before bunking out of town."

"But you seemed pleased that Birdie was adamant about the movie people not setting foot on her land. I saw you smiling when you walked away."

Another nasty smirk twisted his face. "Making lemonade out of lemons. With Dominic no longer in a position to pry his aunt out of her home and her digging in her heels, I'm confident I can convince Pavlova to choose my land for their location. And once Birdie realizes she can't continue without a man about the house, so to speak, I'll make her an offer she can't refuse." He shrugged a beefy shoulder. "Think about it. It would've been to my advantage to negotiate with Dominic, not his aunt. As a businessman, killing him would be counterproductive. And I'm a businessman first and foremost. So if you're looking for a killer, I suggest you shove that stickybeak of yours in another direction. Like that snooty little madam over yonder."

I turned in the direction he'd wobbled his double chin.

April Bradford, market bag hooked over her shoulder, held up a honeydew melon and studied it with the intensity of an artist about to tackle a still life in oils. Guess one couldn't forage for melons in the wild.

"April? You can't mean her. She wouldn't hurt a fly."

"Even a mouse will bite when cornered." He nodded over at her. "And April's no mousie, I'll tell you that for free. I saw her and Dominic having a right dustup in the MacKenzie orchard a few weeks back. Couldn't hear what they were fighting over, but it looked to me as if she was about to take a swing at him with her bag of weeds. Wouldn't have surprised me if she'd stashed a few rocks in the bottom of the bag before she did; she looked mad as a cow stung by a bee. Or maybe a hornet—a *murder* hornet." With a dour chuckle at his own joke, he brushed past me, hollering orders to his minions.

I didn't find Marcus's joke half as entertaining as he did. Whatever had made April angry, had she then directed that fury at Dominic in a murderous way?

Only one way to find out...

NINE

"Beautiful day, isn't it?" I slid into a spot beside April and a wonky pyramid of Brussels sprouts.

She started, tossing up the one she'd been holding. Juggler deft, I caught it midair before it could trigger an avalanche of grossness. That I could see a half dozen other snot-green balls in her market bag meant we were unlikely to ever be friends. Just kidding. I'd never judge a sister by the produce she eats, even if Brussels sprouts really are the devil's bollocks in vegetable form.

"You nearly gave me a heart attack." April slapped a palm to the front of her T-shirt, drawing my attention to the screen-printed slogan emblazoned on it: a crossed-out movie camera and the words 'Keep the Cape Green!'

"Oops. Sorry." I wasn't, not entirely. Curious, though. I hadn't sneaked up on her with my usual panther-like stealth —don't laugh—and she seemed a tad...spooked.

Her eyes darted around as if searching for an escape route.

I plunged ahead, counting on social politeness to keep her from fleeing while I made small talk. "You're up bright and early. Taking a break from cleaning Birdie's house, huh?"

She flinched as though I'd accused her of stealing instead of spring-cleaning. Then her defensive expression settled into a more neutral one. "It's a lot of house for an elderly woman to keep on top of, especially when she's got the animals to look after too. I don't mind helping her out. She can't very well invite people around after the funeral if the place is a mess."

"It's terribly kind of you. Not many people would offer to do the unpleasant but practical tasks that need doing after someone dies. I'm sure Birdie appreciates having a spotlessly clean home." I set the snot-ball sprout on the pyramid's apex, where it wobbled precariously. "Maybe I'm speaking out of turn here, but I don't imagine Dominic helped much with housework."

April's nose crinkled. "His room was an absolute pigpen. Dirty cups and plates, stinky clothes, and junk-food wrappers. It was even worse than my teenage nephew's, and that's saying something."

I made a sympathetic grimace of disgust. "What a man-child. I feel bad for the cops that had to comb through his stuff."

"Totally. They must've had to decontaminate themselves afterward. Yuck." She gave an exaggerated shudder. "I had to take a hot shower to get the feeling of grime off my skin, and I only chucked all the trash on the floor into garbage bags. The room was a fire hazard and a smorgasbord for vermin."

"Nothing of any value hidden under the junk?" I kept my tone light. "I guess the cops are still thinking it was a robbery gone wrong."

"Good luck to any burglar trying to find anything of

value in that dump." She plucked the sprout that I'd carefully balanced off the pile and dropped it into her bag. "Tight-fisted loser. Do you know he made his aunt pay for everything? Groceries, petrol, the electricity bill—all of that and more, according to Birdie. Who treats people like that? If he were alive, I'd tell him exactly what sort of man I thought he was."

"Didn't you confront him a few weeks ago? In Birdie's orchard, remember?" I prompted when April's jaw sagged.

She closed her mouth with a snap and hugged the market bag close to her chest, the sprouts roiling around inside. "Who told you that?"

Despite not owing Marcus Hall any loyalty, I chose to keep his name out of it. "The MacKenzie orchard's right next to the back of the Hall property. Someone saw you and Dominic from there."

Her eyebrows arrowed together in a sharp 'V.' "I bet it was one of those seasonal workers who should be picking apples instead of eavesdropping on other people's private conversations."

"It was described to me as more of an argument than a conversation. What were you arguing about?"

April sniffed and thrust back her shoulders. "Surely your source blabbered all the details."

"They couldn't hear. But they did say you were clearly upset." Carefully monitoring her reaction, I noted her deep exhale and the drop of her shoulders as the tension appeared to melt from them.

"I *was* upset. Birdie's always allowed me and my fellow foragers to collect apples that fall on the ground. She trusted that we'd take only the bruised or damaged fruit, but Dominic accused me of stealing." April huffed through her nose. "Then he had the audacity to order me off MacKenzie land and said if he ever saw me or my foragers on it again, he'd call the cops."

"Wow. That must've made you incredibly angry."

"It did. And I called him a few choice names I won't repeat in public." Her mouth twisted. "It wasn't even his land to begin with, the creep. Not that he seemed to pay much mind to who did own it." She straightened her Keep the Cape Green T-shirt over her hips, once again drawing my attention to it. "The killer at least inadvertently helped our cause because now Pavlova Productions will have to find another town to wreak havoc on."

"You mean Gavin Schmidt's cause? The one they were protesting about outside Hall's gates Friday morning?"

"Yes. I would've been there too, but Gavin wanted me to pick up the boxes of T-shirts we had printed in Napier. A few of us are setting up a stall to sell them over there." April pointed toward a group unloading a van near the entrance to the parking lot. "Twenty bucks for small and medium sizes; twenty-five for large and extra-large. A hundred percent cotton and they come in three different shades of green."

"Nice," I interrupted before she could start in on laundering instructions or a buy-two-get-one-free spiel. "So are you and Gavin, um...close?" I couldn't think of a more tactful way to put it other than to flat-out ask if the two of them were a boyfriend-girlfriend vigilante duo.

"We're friends—if that's what you mean. Oh..." She must've seen something in my expression as her eyes bugged open. "Oh, gosh, no, nothing like that. I'm in a—I mean, I *was* in a long-distance relationship. And Gavin's been a good friend since it, ah, didn't work out. Definitely nothing more than that, on either side." April shook her head, adamant, or so it would seem. "I really haven't the time to go on about my failed romances..."

Nor did I wish to hear about them. I had enough epic romance fails of my own to chew over. The latest being last night's text message from Oliver, consisting of a cat vomiting up a hairball GIF followed by a question mark emoji. I'd replied with a GIF of a purring cat, then a cartoon figure giving multiple thumbs-up. Weren't GIFs and emojis wonderful? You could conduct an entire meaningless conversation without a word being said—or typed, for that matter.

Heaven forbid we said what we actually meant.

"...if you'll excuse me," April was saying, backing up a step so she could move around me to pay the cashier.

"One more thing." I sidestepped to block her. "Can you think of any protesters—or even maybe someone in your foraging group—that might've had an issue with Dominic?"

April's jaw clamped into a bulged position, kind of like she'd stuffed a tiny green puke-ball into each cheek. "Dominic was an arrogant, conniving liar who didn't give a damn about anyone but himself. All of us had an issue with him. That doesn't mean any of us would cold-bloodedly murder the man."

"Of course not, but..."

"If you want to play the part of Nancy Drew, Tessa, shouldn't you start with the basics? Like, perhaps, who benefits from Dominic's death?" Condescension dripped from her tone like drops of honey. Botulism-contaminated honey.

Yeah, well. April's Nancy Drew snark aside, Birdie had already confessed to her nephew's murder. And while she didn't benefit financially, I was certain that, in the long run, she'd be happier without the big bully around. Marcus Hall seemed the next obvious choice; however, any benefit to him of Dominic's demise seemed a little murkier now that we'd spoken. That left...

Mid-ponder, I noticed April developing a smug, close-lipped smile, almost as if she were telepathically tracking the course of my growing suspicions.

"Cora Rossi," I muttered.

"Interesting that the illegitimate MacKenzie heir should show up right now, don't ya think?" April's smile slipped into a sneer. "With her only rival to the throne conveniently out of the running and a baby on the way, the woman certainly isn't pulling any punches when it comes to preying on Birdie's vulnerability." She stabbed one bitten-to-the-quick fingernail at my chest. *"That's* who you should be talking to."

Then, with a toss of her ponytail, she ducked around me.

Leaving me with an unobstructed view of two doe-eyed kids—a girl of about four or five years old and a boy close to double that. Both staring up at me with unabashed fascination.

"'Scuse me, lady," the girl piped up. "Are you Uncle Ricky's girlfriend?"

"THINK you must have the wrong person, sweetie," I said. "I don't know any Rickys." Although, if the uncle was a blood relative of these gorgeous kids with their curly black hair and dazzling grins, I wouldn't mind copping an eyeful of him.

The boy sighed in the way only older siblings can. "You gotta stop calling Uncle Eric Ricky, Vicky."

The girl—his sister Vicky, I deduced—pouted. "Ricky sounds like Vicky. I like it, and Uncle Ricky says he doesn't mind. So there, dummy-pants."

"Big baby. Waah, waah, waah."

As bickering and escalating childish insults ensued, my brain tried to free up some cells to consider the rhyming Ricky-Vicky riddle. Because, darn it, I was tripping over one of the 'ickys.' Ricky, Vicky...Eric-y? Had the boy said Uncle Eric? And of all the possible uncles of all the kids wandering around the market, surely it couldn't be...?

"Simon. Victoria." A deep voice I instantly recognized came from behind me. Directly behind me.

Of course it did.

Eric Mana was always creeping up on me.

He spoke in rapid Māori to the two kids, who'd immediately zipped their lips on hearing their names. While in no way fluent in New Zealand's other official language, I understood a gentle reprimand when I heard one.

Simon grabbed his sister's hand and tried to pull her away, but Miss Victoria was having none of it. "But I wanna talk to Uncle Ricky's girlfriend."

I heard air being sucked through teeth. "My what?" The question was almost a snarl, but his niece and nephew were obviously comfortable that this dog's bark was worse than its bite.

Under his Cape Discovery Primary School wine-and-navy rugby shirt, Simon's shoulders, which would likely be as broad as his uncle's one day, shrugged. "You said you were getting a coffee before my game, then you pointed at her and said you were gonna have a quick word with your friend."

The kids turned their brown laser-beam eyes back to me.

"She's a girl," Vicky said with authority. "And girl plus friend equals girlfriend."

Smart kid. She had him there.

I sealed a giggle inside my mouth and slid a glance over my shoulder. Eric's spooky gray eyes were invisible behind his wraparound shades, but if I hadn't known for a fact that blushing was physiologically impossible for the detective, then that's what I would have called the reddish stain blotching both cheekbones.

Folding my arms, I half turned toward him with innocently raised eyebrows. "Vicky does know her math, Uncle Ricky."

"Vicky and Ricky. See? It mimes." The young girl flashed me a cherubic smile.

"Rhymes," Simon said, but after a darted glance at Eric's mouth, which was set in a *don't push it* line, refrained from adding anything further. He tugged on her arm instead. "C'mon, there's Mr. Blythe and the others. We'll meet you over on the field, okay, Uncle?"

"Okay. Tell your dad I'll be there soon. Look after your little sister."

"I'm not little, and I look after myself." Vicky stamped a gumboot-clad foot and wheeled around, setting the gauzy fairy wings sprouting from the back of her top fluttering.

Simon gave us a pained *look what I have to put up with* eye-roll before catching Vicky's hand and dragging her between the stalls toward the playing fields.

"Remarkable family resemblance," I teased, watching Eric watch the kids as they made their way over to the other mini rugby players and their coach.

While he focused on them, I took the opportunity to, um, focus on him.

And *oh my word*, as Birdie would say. While Detective

Mana dressed in one of his many suits cut an imposingly handsome figure, Eric Mana in jeans and a wheat-colored fisherman's rib sweater made my palms grow sweaty and my legs as wobbly as a newborn calf's.

"They're remarkable kids." Satisfied that his niece and nephew were safely under adult supervision, he shoved his sunglasses onto his head and cut me a sharp look. "What?"

Guess those proverbial eyes in the back of his head must've noticed me staring.

"I haven't seen you out of your clothes before, is all," I said.

It took a full three beats and a glimmer of amusement in Eric's pale gray eyes for me to register what I'd said compared to what I'd meant to say, which was 'I haven't seen you out of your *work* clothes before,' as in, one of his numerous tailored suits. Heat exploded through me as if I'd snatched a jalapeño chili from the nearest vegetable stall and bitten into it.

"Is that an insult or an invitation?" he asked.

Nothing of the professional man of law appeared in the slow, sexy smile curving his lips. It was all Eric—a confident and *comfortable in his own skin* male, one who was aware the opposite sex found him attractive but unaware of just how devastatingly so. It drew me in. The heady mixture of assurance that lacked arrogance, the warmth and humor concealed beneath an armored veneer. His layers upon layers that made me want to peel him apart like an onion. Only the inevitability of tears kept me from stripping off that first layer of Detective Sergeant Mana.

I mentally dunked my burning cheeks in ice water and turned my face toward the playing fields. "I wasn't aware you had family in Cape Discovery, Detective."

Unable to see his reaction to my shutdown of a

possible flirtation, I nevertheless heard it in his smooth baritone when he spoke. "One of my younger brothers: Jerome."

"Simon and Vicky are his?"

"Yep. Simon's nine, and Vicky turns five next month."

"They're lovely." I sent him a side-eye, only to find him studying me instead of his family on the field. Squelching the butterflies dancing crazily in my stomach, I nodded at the takeout coffees in his hands. "Your coffee must be getting cold."

"Hazard of the job." He sipped from one and made a deep rumbling sound of approval. As if the coffee was caressing him as it slid down his throat.

Gah! How could the noises a man made while sipping a hot beverage make my brain come up with such saucy imagery? I needed to get a grip. "You're off duty, aren't you?"

"I'm never really off duty. Your granddad was a cop; you know how it is."

I nodded. "When we were kids, he and Nana Dee-Dee would take us to Napier for the day, and he'd constantly scan the streets, asking us to identify any potential dangers. Nana Dee-Dee used to tell him to quit acting like he expected assassins to pop out from behind every trash can. We thought it was a wonderful game."

"Mini detectives in training." The warmth returned to his voice. "Are all your siblings as nosy as you?"

"Don't you mean as naturally inquisitive and observant?"

"You can stick a pig in a skirt to pretty it up, but it's still a pig." He chuckled and held up a palm. "And before you kick me in the shins, bad analogy. I apologize. There's nothing piggish about you."

"Glad to hear it. Although pigs' intelligence is often underrated. 'Wilbur was modest; fame did not spoil him.'"

"E. B. White fan?"

I blinked at him. "You've read *Charlotte's Web*?"

"Far too many times to count."

"To your nieces and nephews?"

"On some occasions." He gave me a mysterious smile. "'With the right words, you can change the world.'"

Before I could slot foot into mouth by suggesting he didn't look the type to memorize quotes from classic children's literature, a shrill bleating ring erupted from Eric's hip pocket. He glanced down at the coffee cups in his hands, hissing out an impatient sigh. I held out a hand for one of the coffees, and he gratefully passed it over then dug out his phone.

While he spoke in clipped monosyllables, I tried to keep myself from noticing the way his sweater draped across the breadth of his chest. How it fitted snugly over pec and bicep muscles, then hung a little looser over a washboard-flat stomach...*mmm*.

Eric shoved the phone back into his pocket, and I jerked my gaze upward from the level of his fly. Whatever the call was about must've distracted him as he didn't appear to notice, and this man noticed *everything*.

"Sorry about that," he said, as if we'd actually been sharing a moment when the phone call interrupted.

"Work?" Could the frown lines tracking across his forehead mean anything else?

His gaze skipped back to the playing field. "They've discovered a half-submerged car in the river by the Forest Hill rest area."

And for the first responders to call in an off-duty detective... "With a dead body inside?" As if I needed to ask.

"Yeah. With a deceased person inside." He swore under his breath, ripping his eyes from the kids as they lined up in their teams on the field. Grimacing, he pinned me with a stare. "I hitched a ride with Jerome and the kids while Mari took my car shopping. Do you have your car with you?"

"I do."

"Could you drop me off at the rest area?"

"Sure thing. What are girl-plus-friends for?"

TEN

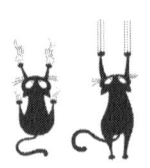

"Does being your civilian driver entitle me to other privileges given to law enforcement agents?" I asked Eric as we drove along beside the river toward Forest Hill Reserve.

"Such as?"

"Getting off a parking infringement?"

"Not police jurisdiction."

"Speeding ticket?"

"You drive like a grandma, so speeding tickets are of little concern."

"That's plain rude. If you weren't a detective, I'd make you get out and walk."

A deep chuckle. "Let me guess. You want the benefit of insider information on the MacKenzie case."

"Can you tell me anything?"

"Other than the investigation's ongoing? Not much."

"Suspects? Marcus Hall, who's never hidden his dislike of Dominic and wants Birdie's land?"

"That's not a crime in itself."

"How about April Bradford? She was seen arguing with the victim. He accused her of stealing their apples."

"Dominic was, by all accounts, the argumentative type, and an accusation of apple larceny is hardly a motive."

Ignoring the amused note in his voice, I continued, "Then there's Cora Rossi, showing up out of the blue and claiming to be Samuel MacKenzie's illegitimate granddaughter. Dollars to donuts she's after some kind of inheritance. That seems a clear motive for getting rid of Dominic."

I shot Eric a glance and found him watching me with a partly admiring, partly irritated expression. "You're as tenacious as a Jack Russell terrier after a rat, aren't you?"

"First, you compare me to a pig, and now a dog? Wow, keep the compliments coming."

"You don't need my approval."

Prickles inched down my spine to cluster in a tight knot around my stomach. I swallowed hard and leaned forward to check my mirrors before overtaking a lumbering motorhome. Once I'd pulled back into the lane and decreased my speed again—this 'grandma' wasn't risking a ticket from the cop next to her regardless of what he said—I slid another glance his way.

"No, I don't need your approval. But maybe, sometime, you might consider me a friend. Friends regard each other as equals."

A sign on the roadside told me the rest area turn off was approaching on the left, so I prepared to signal.

"Friends also don't let friends stumble into dangerous, potentially life-threatening situations. Not if they care about them."

I white-knuckled the steering wheel. *Whoa, now.* Had this big, stoic presence swallowing up every available drop of oxygen inside my car just admitted he cared about me?

Or had that merely been a generalization? I slowed and pulled into the rest area.

Perhaps he just wanted to avoid the inevitable paperwork should a civilian be injured in a homicide investigation.

"You forgot to check your mirrors and signal," Eric remarked as I parked in front of a concrete structure that housed male and female restrooms. "Had you been sitting your driving test, that would've been considered a critical error, and I would have failed you."

"My bad, Detective." I recognized the deflecting humor in his tone, as I often employed this technique after putting my proverbial foot in my mouth. If it hadn't been for the three other marked police vehicles parked nearby and the Hi-Vis vested cops prowling around the rest area, I might not have let him off the hook. Not to mention the unfortunate soul in a ruined car somewhere over the steep bank leading down to the river.

I undid my seat belt, but Eric's warm hand closed over mine before I could remove it from the clip. My questioning gaze flicked up to his deadly serious one.

"You're not getting out of the car, Tessa."

An attempt to pull my hand away failed, his grip tightening only fractionally but enough to still my struggle.

"A person is dead," he said, "and this is a police matter."

I narrowed my eyes at the number of officers outside. Calling out this many cops suggested something much bigger than a simple car going off the road—and in front of the damaged foliage where the vehicle must've gone over the bank, there were no skid marks to indicate an uncontrolled plunge.

"And nothing to do with Dominic MacKenzie," Eric added after a heartbeat.

Call me a cynic, but I didn't quite believe him. My Spidey-senses were tingling.

"Okay," I said in a *compliant good-girl* voice. "Do you think it'll be okay if I use the ladies' room before I drive back to town?" I flashed him my best 'embarrassed but urgency overrides pride' smile. "I need to tinkle."

He snorted out a laugh and released my hand to unclip his own seat belt. "Sure. I'll ask one of the female officers to accompany you."

Huh. A chaperone to use the loo. Obviously, Eric didn't trust me not to wander off on my own. And unfortunately, that meant he understood me better than I'd anticipated.

Before I could protest, the detective climbed from the car and strode over to a cluster of officers, who immediately straightened their shoulders and looked suitably solemn. A female officer soon broke away from the group and beckoned for me to follow. With short strawberry blonde hair and a redhead's pale complexion, she also possessed the accompanying freckles, which covered every inch of her face. While hurrying after her, I tried to keep half an eye on Eric as, along with two other officers, he edged down the bank on a path cut through the weeds by generations of travelers cooling their feet in the river.

"Lovely day today." I assumed the role of 'friendly person making polite chitchat as they prepared to evacuate their bladder whilst accompanied by a police guard.'

"Not for the dead man," the woman said dourly, gesturing for me to enter the ladies' room ahead of her.

Cops and their black humor.

And now I knew the deceased's gender.

Standing inside the cool concrete shelter, I swiveled to face her as she stood braced in the doorway. "No day's a good day to be murdered in your own car and shoved into a river."

Her blue eyes widened. "The detective told you the victim was bludgeoned to death?"

I shrugged and waved my crossed first and second fingers at her. "Eric and I are like this."

Those same blue eyes narrowed into pale-lashed slits.

Hairy yarn *balls*. I'd pushed too hard.

She folded her arms over her Hi-Vis vest and, with one hand, mimicked my crossed fingers. "Detective Sergeant Mana isn't like *this* with anyone. Now, please use the facilities, ma'am."

After offering an apologetic grimace, I scurried into a stall at the far end and latched the door. As luck would have it, for once, I actually didn't need to tinkle, so I quietly lowered the toilet lid and sat on it. In case Officer Freckles crouched down to check.

I made a production of unspooling toilet paper, but those Foley effects couldn't go on for more than twenty seconds without appearing weird. So I sat and stared at the stall door. Contemplating why Eric was lying, why Shelley P. sucked eggs, and whether Tara still loved Cody.

"Not hearing any action in there, ma'am," came an impatient female voice from the other side of the restroom.

"Performance anxiety," I yelled back. "Won't be long."

A bark of male laughter came from Officer Freckles' direction. Did they honestly think having a guy around would make me pee *faster*?

However, on hearing the murmur of lowered voices, I came to the conclusion they were no longer worried about whether I'd gotten over my *urinating for an audience* nerves. Briefly wishing for a disinfecting wet wipe, I pressed an ear to the side of the stall. I couldn't hear what the male officer was saying—always harder to eavesdrop on a man's lower register than a woman's—but I caught a few words Freckles repeated.

Alastair Brown.

Sometime last night.

Gun.

Bundles of cash.

MacKenzie.

Big hairy yarn *balls*. Was Alastair Brown some hitman? A hitman who'd been bludgeoned to death...possibly with the gun he'd used to kill Dominic MacKenzie?

I began to shake, and suddenly, I did need to pee.

WHILE MY BRAIN whirred madly and spun from one thought to another, I spent the rest of Sunday cleaning our apartment. Much like a crazed Roomba bumping into a chair leg over and over, I just couldn't stop thinking about Alastair Brown. Whoever he was.

I'd confessed all to Harry when I arrived home, and in his loving, former-cop way, he'd ordered me to zip it and not talk to anyone about what I'd overheard. Until he could use his contacts to find out more detail, that was.

Early cop gossip was that Alastair Brown, currently unemployed, had died somewhere between nine and ten the previous night. Apparently, as the result of a blunt impact injury to the head, most likely caused by the handgun found in the front passenger footwell. The gun was of the caliber used in the murder of Dominic MacKenzie. Also discovered in the back footwell—a sports bag containing ten thousand dollars cash in mixed denominations. Not much else had been revealed about the man since the police were only just launching their inquiry and investigating any possible connection to the MacKenzie case.

Local officers had already begun canvassing around town with an enlargement of Alastair Brown's driver's license photo. Displaying no bias toward the assumption that a man like Alastair would frequent a yarn store, Officer Jeremy Austin knocked on our back door late that afternoon.

I stared intently down at the image of a man with short gingery hair, insipid blue eyes, and thin lips frozen in a perpetual scowl. "Haven't seen him before, sorry."

"Is this the best photo you could find?" Harry grumbled beside me, frown lines furrowing his brow under his beanie du jour: olive green crochet with alternating thin white stripes. "Couldn't his family give you a better one?"

Jeremy grimaced. "Didn't have much family to speak of. Mother died when he was young. Father's been in and out of prison and hadn't spoken to his son in years. According to his cousin—the only other relative we've been able to unearth—Alastair's been in foster care his whole life. He kept to himself, but the man said the teenage Alastair had some brushes with the law. The cousin thought he'd sorted himself out in the past few years."

This is why Harry's such an asset to my snooping and maneuvering around the thin blue line. Cops tell stuff to other cops, even those who retired years ago. Honestly, it should be Harry trying to find out who'd gotten rid of Birdie's nephew—and then her nephew's killer. Because there was no doubt in my mind that the one person was responsible for both.

An hour after Officer Austin left, there was another knock on our back door. Accompanied by my two inquisitive felines, I opened it to none other than Oliver Novak.

Clutching an extra-large pizza box.

The delicious aroma emanating from it earned him Kit and Pearl's instant adoration. Twining around his ankles, Pearl occasionally hooking a claw or two into the legs of his jeans to encourage him to share, the cats welcomed him to our humble abode.

I, on the other hand, wasn't so forthcoming.

Despite the pizza smelling amazeballs and my stomach teetering on the brink of rumbling like a concrete mixer, I gave him my cheeriest *hey there, neighbor* smile then shouted over my shoulder, "Harry—did you butt-dial pizza again?"

"Nope. But since it's here, pay the delivery kid and bring it on up. I'm wasting away here, waiting for you to cook dinner."

When I turned back, Oliver's initial smile of greeting had dulled into confusion. Give the man props for his inherent male ego, though, as within the space of a heartbeat, his cocky smile reappeared. "Thought you might be hungry after the day you've had," he said.

"I've had a great day. Beginning with the farmers market and sharing a coffee with a good-looking man." Technically true, given that Eric had donated his brother's coffee to me en route to the rest area. A tingle of pleasure in my chest as a flicker of consternation passed over Oliver's face. "Followed by a bit of an adventure with driving to a crime scene and then a burst of spring-cleaning—always food for the soul." Or those requiring a mundane activity to keep themselves from overthinking, well, everything.

He lifted the box higher as Kit stretched up on his back paws and swiped at it. "So, just another uneventful Sunday in the life of Tessa Wakefield?"

"Correct." Again offering a polite-neighbor smile, one

that showcased the result of two years spent in braces. Which reminded me, I must reassure April about what a difference orthodontics could make. "How much do I owe you, delivery kid?"

His head tilted to one side. "Are you mad at me about yesterday afternoon?"

"Don't worry about her, Ollie," came Harry's voice from the foot of the stairs, directly behind me. "She's not mad at you, just hangry. C'mon in, there's beer in the fridge. Nothing like a cold one with a hot slice, am I right?"

"When you're right, you're right." Oliver raised an eyebrow as if requesting my permission to enter.

Tempted to shut the door in his face or claim I had a pre-planned dinner date—sadly, I didn't, unless you counted Netflix—I opted for a shrug and leaving Oliver on the doorstep. "I'll get plates."

Ignoring Harry's frown at my mini rudeness, which would've earned me one of Mum's lectures on being a good hostess, I climbed the stairs to the apartment.

Behind me came the murmur of male voices and the pitiful mewing of greedy cats, who could no doubt identify every individual pizza topping and wanted them all. I placed three dinner plates on the kitchen table, perhaps setting them with a tad more force than was needed. While fetching paper napkins from the pantry, I gave myself a stern talking to.

I wasn't mad at Oliver. *Lie*.

I'd misunderstood the situation. *True*.

My ego was still intact as I hadn't embarrassed myself further. *Partial lie*.

And because I'd read too much into his 'Can I ask you out to dinner sometime when half the pub isn't eavesdropping?'—*true*—like Oliver, I'd changed my mind about wanting us to be anything more than friends. *Complete and utter lie-bomb.*

Yet I still managed to sit with Harry and Oliver and eat pizza as if an actual functioning grown-up person. Even though the jumble of emotions ricocheting around inside made the slice taste like mozzarella-topped polystyrene.

When Harry paused in his verbal dissection of last night's televised game to take a sip of beer—don't ask me what sport; I was too focused on over-chewing my pizza crust—I lunged at the opportunity to change the topic. "Did the boys in blue show up at yours this afternoon?"

Oliver cut me a wary glance, perhaps noting that this was the first time I'd made direct eye contact with him since he'd sat down. "Yeah. Jeremy was asking about that Alastair Brown."

"Did you recognize him from the photo?" I peeled a circle of pepperoni off my slice and nibbled at it. *Très* nonchalant. Until I felt a drip of oil land on my chin.

Oliver lifted a shoulder, and I couldn't help but notice the smooth bulge of muscle moving beneath his shirt. Blinking and ordering myself not to lick my lips, I glanced away.

"I recognized him because he sat not three feet away from me last night," he said.

"At your bar? You were working?"

"Until closing time."

"What was he doing?" The oil slid its way down my chin, so I snatched up a paper napkin and blotted it before it could waterfall off onto my relatively clean T-shirt. "Did you speak to him?"

"Only to take his order. He drank his beer, scrolled on his phone, and kept watching the door like he was expecting someone. I lost track of him. We were busy."

Harry, who'd never seen the point of a napkin when a shirt sleeve would do the trick, swiped his wrist across his mouth and leaned forward in his chair. "And did any unusual 'someones' turn up last night?"

"Some of the Pavlova people were there later in the evening. It must've riled up a table filled with that protester group because three of them—guy with a ponytail, a woman with braces, and another woman who was knitting what looked like a flesh-colored..." Oliver winced. "Never mind. She was knitting something. She and the other two got all up in the Pavlova peoples' business, so I had to tell them to settle down, or I'd throw them out."

Oh, gee whiskers. I knew someone who liked to knit flesh-colored...*things*. Sounded like Nadia must be walking close to the wild side again—and from Oliver's descriptions, Gavin and April weren't discouraging it. My mind drifted toward possible conversation starters aimed at opening a dialog where I gently steered Nadia's passions toward a healthier, more-lawful way of expressing herself. I hauled it back to the present and the young man they'd found dead in his car that morning.

"Did you notice anyone talking to Alastair?" I asked. Then tried not to notice how cute Oliver looked when he was thinking hard. Along with the twist of his kissable lips—*now where the heck had that come from?*—he lightly tugged on the scruff along his jaw.

"Hang on—yeah. When I returned from a break, I saw him talking to a woman. He appeared to be flirting with her or attempting to while she waited for Lucinda to fix her virgin margarita. The woman was giving off 'I'm out of your league' vibes left and right, but the poor guy didn't seem to notice." Oliver gave a rough but sympathetic chuckle. "You'd think he might've guessed she was pregnant, if not by her choice of cocktail, then by the belly under her dress. But maybe that wasn't much of a deterrent, given that she wasn't wearing a wedding ring."

Huh? My fingers loosened on the pizza slice, and I let it fall to the plate. Who had I met yesterday evening that was pregnant and attractive?

Harry snorted. "If she was pretty enough that you noticed she wasn't wearing a ring, I'm sure this Alastair character must have too. Bit of a looker, was she?"

As Oliver's gaze shot to mine, I raised a *well, was she?* eyebrow.

Caution tautened his voice. "Yeah."

"Dark hair, dark eyes, looks like a pregnant supermodel?" Confession: I had to keep a tight rein on my tongue to prevent even an ounce of snark from slipping off of it.

"Uh-huh."

"Who do you know like that?" Harry asked, then his face cleared. "Wait a sec. Didn't you tell me Sam's granddaughter was in the family way?"

"*Alleged* granddaughter," I mumbled. "And yes, it could have been her Alastair was talking to."

"More like striking out with by the sounds of it." My granddad chuckled and took another sip of his beer.

"And you don't know what time Alastair left?" I asked.

"As I said, we were slammed, but he'd gone by the time Lucinda took her break just before nine."

"The woman definitely didn't leave with him?"

"The last time I saw her, she was sitting at the Pavlova guys' table, chatting with one of the suits." Oliver reached for another pizza slice and started telling Harry about the time an All Black had a few beers at the Stone's Throw.

I wanted to ask if he'd noticed what time Cora Rossi

left. Whether she'd hung around until closing time and left the bar *with him*.

But I didn't.

Because: ouch. Pregnant or not, Cora Rossi was more in Oliver's league than I would ever be. A voice inside me hissed that I couldn't compete with the Cora Rossi's of this world, so why risk a man stomping on my heart again as my ex had?

ELEVEN

STEWART MORRIGAN WAS A FUNERAL DIRECTOR. As was his father, Stewart Senior, the owner of Morrigans Funeral Home in Cape Discovery. And another funeral director, his uncle by marriage, also had the unfortunate first name of Stuart. Though spelled differently, as Uncle Stuart was always quick to point out when meeting potential clients.

Well, the living ones at least.

This wasn't my first introduction to the youngest of the three Stewarts—*Stews?*—as Stewart Junior had been the front man for Nana Dee-Dee's funeral last year. Quietly spoken and impeccably mannered, Stewart had soon charmed my mother and sisters. Dad and me? Let's just say our fancy word of the day to describe him would've been 'obsequious.'

As for Harry's opinion...well, a gorilla dressed in disco flares and gold chains could've run Nana's funeral, and the poor darling wouldn't have noticed.

However, for this morning's meeting, clad in a suitably somber dark-gray suit with coordinating red tie and not a gold chain in sight, Stewart Junior greeted Birdie, Cora, and me in the funeral home's reception with an equally somber expression and handshake.

Yep—you heard me—Cora.

Decked out in slim-fitting black pants and a floaty tunic that flowed over her curves, Cora owned the casual-but-chic look without even breaking a sweat. When I'd turned up this morning, she'd been waiting with Birdie to accompany us to the meeting with Death's PR man. And I could hardly say no when Birdie asked if it would be all right for her to come with us 'as an extra support for me.'

The younger woman had flashed me a *cat plucking canary feathers out of its teeth* smile as she slipped an arm around Birdie's hunched shoulders. "If Tessa objects, I can take my own car and meet you there."

As if I could possibly object now.

I'd dredged up the most gracious expression I could muster and kept it firmly in place as I ushered Birdie and her unexpected houseguest to my car.

"April's not coming?" I'd asked after climbing into the driver's seat.

"Why would she?" Cora's voice came razor-sharp from the back seat. "She's not family." *And neither are you,* her tone implied.

"Oh, April kindly volunteered to shift into Dominic's room when she got home and met Cora. I heard her tapping away on her keyboard after we'd fed the animals this morning, so I guess she must have work to catch up on."

Our drive into the town couldn't end fast enough. However, I made sure to keep below the speed limit, as given the number of extra police in the area, I didn't want to risk attracting their attention.

Stewart ushered us into a tastefully decorated room that reminded me of a stern grandmother's formal parlor. Sofas designed to keep sitters from lingering past their welcome, lots of dark polished wood, framed prints on the walls in soothing colors of algae green and muted blue, and of course, the obligatory boxes of tissues placed on end tables within easy reach of the sofas.

While Cora and I bookended Birdie, Stewart perched on the sofa opposite, looking so much like a cartoon vulture that I had to squeeze my lips together and study my shoelaces.

After discussing the logistics and cost of a small service for her nephew, Birdie left us to accompany the funeral director into a private viewing room to see Dominic's body. Given that Cora seemed to have attached herself to Birdie's side for the foreseeable future, I knew I wouldn't get a better opportunity than this.

But I couldn't just lob a grenade at her like, 'did you happen to have ten thousand dollars cash floating around that you used to pay a hitman?' I understood why I was protective of the woman who'd been one of Nana Dee-Dee's closest friends—*hello*, grief transference—but I realized if I appeared threatening to Cora, she could effectively cut my access to Birdie then carry out whatever devious plan she'd set in motion.

"Did you ever meet your, er, cousin?" I asked, a verbal nod to my acceptance of her as Samuel's legitimate grandchild, calculated to start the subtle campaign of getting her to talk.

Cora, who'd put as much distance between us as possible by hip-butting the rolled arm of the sofa, angled her head toward me. "Once. It wasn't an experience I was eager to repeat."

"It didn't go well?"

"I can't imagine many encounters with that man ever

did. He was quite possibly the rudest human being I've ever met." Her lip curled as she smoothed the mint green folds of gauzy fabric over her baby bump.

Shifting to face her profile, I hooked my ankle under my knee and draped an arm over the sofa back: Open and Interested Body Language 101.

"Just between the two of us"—I lowered my voice to a conspirator's hush—"I'd be surprised if anyone attends this funeral other than Birdie and the people who want to support her. Dominic wasn't well-liked around here."

Cora gave a soft snort. "You don't say."

"Hard to believe, I know. Your cousin being a prince among men, and all."

That earned me a bona fide smile. "He certainly seemed to think he was some sort of king." Cora's smile slipped as her eyes narrowed to slits. "The arrogance of the man. Denying me access to Birdie. Like he had any right to decide whether or not I could speak to her."

I allowed my mouth to drop open. "He did what, now?"

Cora twisted on the sofa, mirroring my pose, so we faced each other across the expanse. I had her now. "I drove up on Easter Friday to introduce myself to Birdie. That wasn't easy, let me tell you."

"Of course it wasn't. It took real guts to put yourself out there when you had no idea how she'd react."

Cora leaned in. "I felt sick about it. I mean, it's not exactly easy to say, 'Excuse me, but your late husband knocked up a girl while you were on a break, and, surprise, I'm his granddaughter.' Also knocked up."

"But you didn't get a chance...?"

She shook her head. "There was a truck about halfway up the driveway, blocking it, so I got out and followed a path between the trees to a clearing."

I'd heard about this clearing from Birdie. One of her nephew's schemes to help cut costs at the cat motel. "Where Dominic was cleaning kitty litter."

"Yes! He was in the middle of hosing down a container of it"—her nose wrinkled as if remembering the stench—"and there was a huge pile inside a shed. Thank goodness that stuff was clean. I think." She waved a dismissive hand. "Whatever. I asked him politely if he could move his truck as I was Mrs. MacKenzie's granddaughter and wanted to visit her."

"Did you know the man you were speaking to was Birdie's nephew?"

"I'd found out she had a nephew, but no, I didn't realize it was him. Until he took one look at me and started yelling that I couldn't speak to his aunt and that he wanted me off the property or he'd throw me off himself."

"He took one *look* at you? Do you think he noticed the similarity between you and his uncle and felt threatened?"

Cora lifted a delicate shoulder. "That was the conclusion I came to while running back to my car as fast as I could. I reversed down to the road and ended up parking in front of the neighbor's driveway, bawling and shaking like a newborn kitten. Pregnancy hormones, gotta love 'em." She rolled her eyes, and I smiled my sisterhood smile of encouragement. "I had no idea what to do next, but then someone tapped on my window."

"The neighbor? Marcus Hall?" I asked.

"Yes. Marcus. That's how he introduced himself. When he asked whether I was lost or needed help, I ended up blurting out what had happened and asking if there was any way he could help me talk to Birdie."

"I don't believe Marcus and Birdie are on the best of terms."

Cora gave me a wry smile. "He told me he couldn't help because both MacKenzies hated him, but perhaps I should hang around for a few days, as 'good things came to those who wait.' Bizarre thing to say, don't you think?"

I didn't get a chance to reply as Birdie and Stewart returned at that moment, Birdie's face only half a shade darker than the Greek yogurt I'd eaten at breakfast this morning. She sat heavily between us and took our hands, squeezing tightly as if trying to prevent herself from floating away.

"I really am alone now, girls," she said and began to weep.

While we rushed to simultaneously hug Birdie and pass her tissues, part of my brain remained reptilian-cool and distant, gnawing over what Cora had revealed.

What *had* Marcus meant by his cryptic comment to a woman he'd discovered was a long-lost member of the MacKenzie clan?

MY BRAIN still mulling over the possibility that the MacKenzies' neighbor might be a cold-blooded psycho who'd paid to have Dominic shot, I drove Cora and Birdie home.

With my attention focused on getting us there without running off the road—the importance of this reinforced by the car-into-the-river incident yesterday morning—it was Cora in the back seat who spotted the police vehicle blocking Marcus Hall's driveway. "Police! Gosh, what's happened now?" she asked no one in particular.

Birdie's chin had sagged to her chest, but at the sound of

Cora's voice, her head popped up. "Oh my word—stop, Tessa, and let's find out."

I pulled over by Marcus's driveway. Safely, mind you, because two officers watched us from beside the marked police car.

Birdie studied the female officer as she strolled toward us. "Why, that's Ivy Smith's granddaughter." She buzzed down the passenger window. "Good morning, Officer. How's that tabby ball of mischief behaving himself?"

The woman's face went from grim to gooey in a heartbeat. "Oh, he's just the sweetest boy. Thank you again for putting the two of us together."

"You were meant for each other." Birdie glanced back over her shoulder at me. "Officer Denton needed a companion, and wee Tigger, who was abandoned as a tiny kitten, needed someone kind and patient to hand rear him."

Officer Denton gave an aw-shucks smile and rested her forearms on the car's sill. "It's Philippa, Birdie. You've known me since Grandma used to tell me off for bringing cicadas and butterflies with broken wings home in my school lunchbox."

Birdie chuckled. "That I have."

Once the two of them had exchanged sympathies and family updates, Birdie patted Philippa's arm. "Now, what's going on up there, honeybunch? Anything we ladies should be concerned about?"

Philippa flicked a glance over her shoulder at her partner, who was surreptitiously checking his phone. When she turned back, unlined brow crumpled under regulation hat. "I can't say much, but once the media arrives, it'll be all over the news anyway." Another quick peek back at the driveway had all three of us leaning toward her in anticipation.

We were well rewarded.

"You know how that man, Alastair Brown, was found dead in his car yesterday?"

We all nodded like Bobbleheads.

"Turns out he picked apples for Marcus two seasons ago."

"Fancy that," Birdie breathed.

Surely that wasn't enough to justify a police presence?

Philippa continued, "While they were searching Alastair's car, they found a burner phone. The call history showed only one cell phone number, and that was another burner phone." Her eyes widened theatrically. "And then multiple calls to a landline—*Marcus Hall's* landline."

"I'm not sure I understand, Philippa dear," Birdie said. "Why would you lot think Marcus killed a young man who used to work for him?"

The young officer's gaze traveled past Birdie and slammed into mine.

I got it. I understood why.

Attempting to moisten a suddenly parched mouth, I ran my tongue around my teeth while watching the cop's-code-of-silence reassert itself on Philippa's face.

She straightened and took a backward step away from the car. "I really can't say anything more without getting into a whole lot of trouble with my superiors."

"We wouldn't want to get you into any trouble," Birdie said.

A beat later, when Officer Philippa's partner hollered her name and gestured at me to move along, the young woman gave us a tight smile and rushed back to rejoin him.

As I cruised along the road, darting frequent glances in my rearview mirror, another police vehicle appeared behind us and waited to turn out of Hall's driveway. This car carried a passenger in its back seat.

Marcus Hall.

Birdie leaned forward to see past me as I made the turn into her driveway. "Is that Marcus? Have they arrested him?"

"Certainly looks that way." Cora untwisted herself from where she'd been staring out the rear window. "I guess we know who's responsible for Dominic's murder."

"Dominic's murder?" Birdie squawked. "I thought they were carting him off to the station for killing the young apple-picking man?"

"Him too," Cora said. "It all makes sense now. Marcus wanted your nephew gone, so he paid this Alastair guy to do his dirty work. He looks like he could easily afford to."

"That he could." Birdie sniffed.

I wondered just how much of the cash he collected at the markets each week found its way into a bank account. It'd be all too easy to skim a little off the top to use however he wanted. Untraceable too.

"Bet he thought that without a man around the place to look after me, I'd fall to pieces and practically gift him the land." Scorn dripped from Birdie's every word. Scorn and stubbornness. If that had been Marcus's plan all along, he'd underestimated the Widow MacKenzie.

"And then he took out Alastair and cleared up his loose ends," Cora said as I parked in front of the house. "Case closed."

Birdie reached over and patted my leg. "We didn't need your powers of deduction after all."

From the back seat came a sharp bark of laughter. "Looks like you dropped the ball on this one, Sherlock. It's all pretty obvious when you think about it."

"Guess you're right." Even though the pit of my stomach felt like it was about to free fall into my shoes, I kept my tone light.

"Let's go inside and have a nice cup of tea," Birdie said.

I let Birdie and Cora get out ahead of me while I spent a moment staring across at the distant line of Hall apple trees. Marcus's guilt seemed obvious, and I knew well the adage about zebras and horses.

However, something niggled at me as I sighed and climbed out of my car. Couldn't quite put my finger on it.

But something definitely niggled.

TWELVE

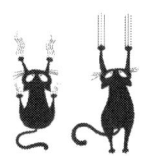

My mission, should I choose to accept it, was to find April up at the Clowder Motel and see if she wanted to join us for a cup of tea. Not a particularly challenging mission because, thanks to the process of elimination, we knew April wasn't in the house.

Leaving Cora and Birdie to potter in the kitchen, I strolled over toward the barn. Birdie had more cats staying this week and had mentioned how grateful she was for the extra business, despite suspecting some people just wanted to gawk at the house where a murder took place. Three of her guests watched me approach, but knowing cats, there were likely at least two more studying me from their hiding spots amongst the foliage.

One of the cats, an elegant black beauty, strolled along a branch and poked its nose through the chicken wire when I held out my fingers for it to sniff. A pang of guilt as he, or she, gave my fingers a token lick. I hadn't paid much attention to Kit and Pearl this past week, and I resolved to have a decent play date with them and their toys this evening.

Distracted by the kitty, who meowed sorrowfully when

I moved away, I didn't think to call out for April but instead just breezed into the barn. Apparently, my ninja skills were better than I realized, or April was so caught up in pulling cleaning supplies down off a shelf that she failed to hear me. With her back to me, she stood on tiptoes on the top rung of a stepladder, patting one hand along a dusty shelf while holding a large bottle of cleaning solution in the other. In case she was even a fraction as clumsy as me, I thought it best not to startle her.

"It must be here. I've looked everywhere else, for Pete's sake." Her fingers connected with something hidden to her eyes, sending an aerosol can plummeting from the shelf to the floor with a clatter.

When April twisted on the stepladder to follow its bouncing trajectory, she spotted me frozen in the doorway and let out a squeak of surprise. But, to give her props, at least she didn't tumble off the stepladder as I would have.

"Tessa!" She clutched at her chest. "You nearly gave me a heart attack."

"Lost something?" I asked faux innocently. "Need a hand looking for it? And when I say *it*, I'm assuming you're looking for something of Dominic's?"

April's knuckles whitened on the cleaning bottle, and plastic crackled. She glanced down at her hand then placed the bottle on the shelf. "That's ridiculous. What would I want with his crappy old laptop? Half the keys didn't work, anyway. It's not worth anything."

Laptop? Who'd said anything about a laptop? Birdie had only listed Dominic's phone and tablet as missing.

In the hopes of finding out why this laptop was so important, I decided to play along.

"You seem to know a lot about a dead man's computer,"

I said as she climbed down from the stepladder. "Especially for a person who supposedly hated him."

April sniffed disdainfully. "I've seen him at Rosie's a few times, pounding away on the keyboard and muttering curses at it."

Interesting. Dominic had a laptop in addition to his other devices. So where was it? One look at April's clamped-together jaw told me it was pointless trying to grill her, even though it was now obvious she'd been searching for his laptop since the very beginning. Time for a change of tack. "Did you know Alastair Brown?"

Small muscles around her mouth tightened, drawing her lips into a cat-butt pucker. "I don't associate with criminals."

Not exactly a denial, but... "I didn't realize he was a criminal. What's he done?"

April shrugged. "A friend of a friend said her brother did prison time with him for burglary, and graduating from burglary to home invasion's not such a stretch. I'm surprised Marcus even hired him, although, given what we now know, it does make a horrible kind of sense."

She stalked toward me, raising a haughty eyebrow. "If you're done giving me the third degree, did you want something?"

"Birdie sent me to find out if you'd like a cup of tea."

The haughty eyebrow dropped, and a mask of politeness descended. "Ah, tea fixes everything, doesn't it?"

I gestured for her to go out ahead of me, taking the opportunity to run my gaze over the barn for one last look. Nothing appeared out of place.

That niggle again.

Why risk prison time when Mother Nature will take care of things for me? Marcus had said.

Marcus Hall might be many things, but stupid wasn't one of them. Killing Alastair and then leaving evidence connected directly to him wasn't only risky; it was plain stupid.

FIRST ORDER OF BUSINESS, after chin scratches with the kitties and apologizing to Harry for once again leaving him in sole charge of the store, was to promise my granddad an extra muffin from the Daily Grind. I sent Rosie a text asking if she'd sacrifice her lunch break to talk to me.

ROSIE: I can spare twenty for coffee and a salted caramel and cashew muffin. My boss had her baby brother over for a slumber party last night so she's a cranky witch this morning.

ROSIE'S BOSS SOUNDED DREADFUL. Shame she was self-employed.

ME: Sorry, but are you complaining about Archie? The cutest baby in the history of babies? I stopped paying attention after salted caramel and cashew muffin.

ROSIE REPLIED with an eye-roll emoji and an order to arrive in our usual lunch spot at quarter past one.

We met around the back of her café, at the picnic table used by staff for their breaks when the weather allowed. As it was a little chilly today, I found Rosie waiting with a couple of the crocheted afghans she'd commissioned me to make for customers who sat out front in the cooler months. Also awaiting me was a steaming to-go cup, a wickedly decadent looking muffin on a plate, and two paper takeout bags, which I'd bet contained a few more muffins. Rosie could protest we weren't real friends until the cows came home, but those extra muffins spoke for themselves.

"How goes it, bestie?" I teased, taking the bench seat opposite and snuggling under the chunky wool afghan.

"Shut up and eat that muffin before I do. I've already weakened and succumbed to a second one today, and if I go for a third, my mother will ramp up her hints about me joining her weight-loss program."

I eyed Rosie's teenager-cheerleader physique, refusing to glance down at my quarterback-worthy thighs. "Is that the one held at St Barney's Hall on Wednesday nights? 'Your Body: His Temple'?"

"Yeah," Rosie muttered with a frown. "Eunice is now their poster child after transforming from 'fat and fifty' to 'fabulous and fifty.' She suckered my mum right in."

"Well, the day my temple does the walk of shame into St Barney's hall on a Wednesday night is the day I give you permission to cut me off cold turkey from your baked goods."

Just to spite the vicar's wife, I broke off a generous chunk of muffin and stuffed it into my mouth. Eunice Salmon had no idea what she was missing. Sheer mini orgasm in a bite.

But perhaps orgasms weren't allowable in a pearl-clutcher's worldview.

"Anyway, since your boss is such a witch today, maybe we should discuss giving up muffins another time."

"Preach it, girlfriend." Rosie reached over and stole a corner of my muffin. "FOMO; can't help it. So, what's up?"

In between mouthfuls of ecstasy, I filled her in, finishing with my discovery of April searching the barn for Dominic's old laptop. Her head cocked like a small curious bird, Rosie listened while sipping her coffee.

"She always was a cagey little thing in high school. Scurrying from class to class, loitering in the library. Do you remember her?" she asked once I was done.

On some level, I knew we'd attended the same high school, but I'd spent most of my years there with my head down, buried in my books. I didn't remember April, not at all. She might as well have been invisible, and a twinge of guilt had me shifting uncomfortably on the bench seat.

I shook my head. "Nope. She'd have been a few years behind us. What about Dominic? Was he one of your regulars?"

"Not really. But I've seen them both in here, working on their computers," she said. "And yes, Dominic's looked ancient."

"Have you seen April and Dominic together, I mean, here at the same time?"

Rosie frowned in concentration. "No, I don't think so. And until recently, April was too busy looking at her screen to notice anyone else in the café."

"How so?"

"Well, I don't make a habit of spying on customers, but a few times she's been in here, giggling and blushing while staring at her laptop screen. Once, when I delivered her coffee, I noticed she was on a dating website—what's it called? Kiwi-Match, no—KiwiConnect."

"And being a married woman, you'd know this how?"

That earned me a long-suffering sigh. "I'm married, not

dead. A friend of Brad's met his girlfriend on there. That Australian girl who's just moved in with him. You met her at our Saint Patrick's Day party, remember?"

I felt my eyes bug. "They met on KiwiConnect?"

"Yeah, funny story. She sent him a decade-old photo of herself, and he sent her one taken twelve years ago. You can imagine their surprise when they eventually met at Auckland International. Luckily, they liked each other anyway."

"Huh. Kind of catfishing." My suspicious mind conjured up images of April flirting with Alastair online and then finding out he wasn't a smooth-talking, charming bachelor but a former inmate. "Any idea who April was chatting with on KiwiConnect?"

"My superhero vision isn't as awesome as yours, so I couldn't read the name on her chat screen. But I did see his photo."

I quickly finished chewing my muffin chunk and leaned forward. "Did he have shifty eyes, red hair, and look as if he could use a few decent meals?"

Rosie's nose crinkled. "Ew, *no*. He was blond, clean-cut, and looked more like a stock photo that would come up if you typed 'good-looking blond man in his thirties' into a search engine." She raised her eyebrows. "Another thing—and I know this makes me sound like the mean girl I used to be—but the guy in the photo was just too hot, *too* perfect."

Part of me bristled. The part that had, for a moment, thought someone as hot and perfect as Oliver Novak might be interested in an average woman, flaws and all.

Gah! I needed to stop projecting my baggage onto murder-suspect stuff.

"Don't get your back up, Tess," Rosie said. "I'm not saying the guy was too attractive for April. I'm saying the man she was chatting with might not have been who she thought he was. Even a five-year-old knows how to search and copy a photo from the Internet."

I took a moment to digest that, along with another mouthful of divinity. "When did you last see April making goo-goo eyes at her laptop?"

"Must be a couple of weeks ago now," Rosie said. "Maybe the online thing with Mr. Perfect didn't work out."

I doubted Mr. Perfect or April's love life had anything to do with the two recent murders in Cape Discovery, so I circled back to my original reason for wanting to meet with Rosie. Other than her generosity with baked goods, of course. "Do you know if April knew Alastair Brown?" At her blank look, I added, "The guy killed in his car."

She pulled a face. "I know who you mean. You're not the only business owner in town to get a visit from the smokin' Detective Mana."

I chose not to point out that the detective hadn't graced Unraveled with his presence but had instead sent Jeremy with his clipboard. Sad when you felt a prick of jealousy because a homicide detective delegated the task of dealing with an annoying pain-in-his-butt civilian to an underling. I had only myself to blame for that. Call it a psychotic need for resolution and closure. "Did you recognize him? Was he a customer?"

"Eh." Rosie made a seesaw motion with her hand. "Like I told the detective, the odds of me remembering a customer that I may or may not have served a couple of years ago are about the same as me remembering one of the guys Brad used to play Dungeons and Dragons with back in the day. Before I beat the geek out of him." She leaned forward, her smile sharpening from *happily married mother of three* to *psychotic pixie* in an instant. "And as I also told the detective, while I didn't recognize Alastair Brown as a customer, I do remember seeing him and April at Davy Jones on Valentine's Day a couple of years ago." She sat back and folded her arms, waiting for me to take the bait she knew I couldn't resist.

Davy Jones was one of Cape Discovery's restaurants. It wasn't the most expensive place to eat in town—that would be the Seafarer, where you had to make a reservation, and they used *real* cloth napkins. And it wasn't the cheapest—that would be the Jade Blossom, with an order-by-number menu and dusty decor à la nineteen seventies kung fu movies. Davy Jones was a 'middle-of-the-road married couple who didn't need to impress each other with fine dining and young couple who did but couldn't afford a thirty-dollar entrée' type of place.

"Brad was splashing out, huh?"

"You betcha. For a night out with no kids, I'd have been thrilled with a Happy Meal and a chocolate sundae. Anyway, while Alastair wasn't on my radar at the time, April was. She was my Triple-Soy-No-Sugar-No-Foam-Latte who came in Monday, Wednesday, and Friday mornings, regular as clockwork. On my way to the ladies' at Davy Jones, I noticed her and that guy in the cops' printout sitting at a table. Couldn't swear on a stack of Bibles they were on a date, but it was the first time I'd seen her in a dress and out from behind her laptop screen."

"April organizes the forager group, so she must put down the electronics sometimes."

"She wasn't foraging at the restaurant." Rosie screwed her mouth into a sympathetic grimace. "Unless it was for sparkling conversation. If they were on a date, it didn't appear to be going well."

"What was he doing?"

"Working on his interested face as April described her

latest foraging walk, where one of the walkers lost a gumboot to a particularly muddy puddle." She shrugged. "April must've followed me into the ladies' because we ended up washing our hands at the same time and made awkward eye contact in the bathroom mirror. I left the restroom just after her too, so I was close enough to see her reaction when she returned to an empty table. The guy's jacket, which he'd draped over the back of his chair, was gone. As were his wallet and phone. Wouldn't surprise me if he'd stiffed her with the check too."

"He bailed on her? What a dick."

"A whole bag of them. April paid and left without finishing her meal."

"On a scale of one to ten, how devastated was she?"

Rosie stole my last chunk of muffin and chewed it while contemplating her answer. Eventually, she brushed crumbs off her fingers and met my gaze. "I didn't really see devastation on her face—April looked furious. The kind of furious that makes a woman take a baseball bat to her cheating man's car."

Or whack him upside the head with a gun?

I thanked Rosie for the coffee and muffins and let her get back to her caffeine-deprived customers in need of a fix.

As I walked home, I tried to put myself in April's shoes. If Oliver had ditched me mid-first date, would I have waited two years for revenge? Rather an over-the-top payback. You'd have to be more than a little unhinged to carry that out. But the unhinged walked among us, wearing carefully crafted suits of normality. It was only under those suits that some sported their super-villain spandex onesies.

Was April one of them?

I waved across the road to Donna Hanbury of Hanburys grocery store. She returned the gesture then mimed pouring something into an imaginary glass and drinking it. Wine o'clock, for sure.

Though maybe not at the Stone's Throw.

Which reminded me. On the night Alastair died, Oliver had seen April in his pub, causing trouble with the protester group. Had she spotted her runaway date trying to chat up another woman and dealt out the justice of a woman scorned?

Possible, I guessed. Then again, April had been seen in a public place, which gave her an alibi. But was it airtight?

THIRTEEN

As a rule, Monday and Tuesday mornings were busy at Unraveled, with customers coming in to restock supplies depleted over the weekend. Thanks to a misty drizzle that threatened an imminent downpour, this particular Tuesday morning had started out slow; however, I was as snug as a bug in a rug while Kit and Pearl snoozed in their beds beside the cash register. The duo had poked their noses outside earlier, scented rain in the air, and sensibly decided to catch up on their napping schedule.

When the bell above the door jingled, I looked up from where I sat on one of the store's armchairs, working on a fuchsia pink cowl for Rosie's birthday next month. In a luxurious cashmere yarn that cost an arm and a leg. Am I an awesome friend or what?

A rhetorical question because my brain simply stopped functioning at the sight of Eric striding into the store. Eric, dripping wet, his white business shirt transparent against his tanned chest, revealing so many ridges and valleys of muscle that it made me want to take up mountain climbing.

Forget the competition; Detective Sergeant Mana had my vote in a wet T-shirt contest.

He held two takeout coffees in his hand, one balanced on top of the other.

"I should arrest the barista for superheating his coffee to the point of third-degree burns on my fingertips," Eric said by way of greeting.

He must've noticed my eyes focused at chest level and assumed I was wondering why the balancing act. Spoiler alert: I wasn't. I just couldn't drag my gaze from the wet, clingy, and very fine cotton. Or was it him that was fine? *Oh so very fine.*

I glanced down at the cowl and the three stitches I'd managed to drop from my needles. Then tossed the cowl into the basket beside the chair and stood. Ashamed to admit it, but my legs were a tad wobbly as I made my way over to the display baskets sitting on the counter. "Just so happens I have something for that very problem."

Crocheted cup cozies in hand, I circled the counter and relieved Eric of the top takeout cup. "Here." I slid the gray wool sleeve over it and offered it to him. We swapped, and I did the same to the second cup with a black sleeve.

When I went to return that one, Eric held up a hand. "That's yours."

"Wow. You bought me a coffee?" I blurted, real sophisticated-like.

"You don't appear to function well without it." A dimple puckered his cheek, the precursor to an actual smile. Not that I got one. Instead, he offered a scowl as he plucked his wet shirt away from his skin. It made a juicy sucking sound, wrenching my gaze toward the man's chest once again.

I cleared my throat, focusing on Pearl's jaw-stretching

yawn and slit-eyed suspicion of this damp human intruding on her personal space. "Can I get you a towel?"

"Please. And one for the floor. I'm creating a slip hazard."

Abandoning him to Pearl's disdain, I hightailed it upstairs to retrieve some towels. I grabbed the first couple off the stack and raced back down to the store. Eric hadn't moved, but I had to swallow a grin at the sight of him—one hand braced on his hip as he majestically sipped his coffee under the unwavering stares of two black cats.

When I tossed over the first towel, he caught it with his hip-hand like an old-time gunslinger. He dropped it to the floor and swirled it around in the puddle forming at his feet. The second towel he caught just as nimbly, and I enjoyed the show of him rubbing down his hair and chest while I tested out my coffee.

Perfection. Just like him.

I leaned against the counter and crossed my ankles. "Call me cynical, but why have you come bearing gifts?"

His eyebrow twitched upward. "I thought enabling each other's caffeine addiction was kind of our thing."

Coffee was our thing? And here's me thinking awkward encounters and me nearly getting arrested was our thing. However, I decided not to look a gift horse in the mouth, even one with such pedigree.

"Well, thank you." I toasted him with my cup. "So purely a social call?"

The dimple reappeared. Then immediately vanished. "Not entirely."

Hazarding a guess, I set my cup down. "Marcus?"

"We had to release him. He lawyered up immediately, and his lawyer got him out on a technicality. He'll be home by now."

I wrapped my arms around my waist, hoping Eric wouldn't notice the shiver working its way down my spine. "Do you think he did it? I mean, off the record. Did he pay Alastair Brown to do it?"

"Off the record, yeah." He scrubbed the towel over his face, and when he dropped it again, his eyes were frozen chips of concrete. "But we've more work to put in before we can arrest him."

"You must find that incredibly frustrating."

"All part of the job." He cleared his throat. "It's a sucky part of the job, but we'll be better prepared next time we take a run at him."

And from the flash of bared, white teeth, which one could've described as a grin if it weren't so damn scary, you could have paid me a king's ransom, and I still wouldn't want to be in Marcus Hall's shoes when Detective Mana caught him.

Or maybe I would.

"If there's anything I can do to help…" I uttered the clichéd phrase before my brain had fully returned from the image of Eric patting me down against a wall.

He pinched a spot between his eyebrows. "No. Please, no."

When he next looked at me, the ice had melted, but his gaze was no less hard and determined. "You need to keep away from Marcus. He's a suspect in a double homicide, and although innocent until proven guilty, I don't want you anywhere near him."

"Because I could screw up the case you're building. Yeah, yeah, I get it."

"I'm not sure you do."

He stalked across the store, quiet and light on his feet in a way Kit could only dream of, and came to a halt in front of me. Close enough for his cologne to tickle my nose; close enough to notice a ridge of scar tissue peeking out from beneath the two opened buttons of his shirt.

Eric leaned in, and my throat constricted, blood rushing to my cheeks. *Oh, wow*. His lips were full and firm. Should I close my eyes and pucker up? Typical, today of all days, I'd skipped the mouthwash, but thankfully I hadn't had onions for breakfast, and...

He set his coffee cup next to mine and straightened, but before I could breathe a sigh of relief that I hadn't tried to sneak a quick breath-check and assumed the *kiss me, you fool* simper, he gripped me by the upper arms. The shock of his touch, even though I only imagined the heat of his fingertips burning through my sweater, stopped my heart the way plunging into the ocean on a winter's day would do.

"Twice now, I've found you in a killer's crosshairs—after the fact. You could have been seriously hurt. Or worse." A fingertip stroked up and down my arm. "I don't want to arrive too late to a crime scene and find you the star of it. I just couldn't bear..." His Adam's apple yo-yoed against the rasp of his strained swallow.

After we'd stared at each other for what felt like the time equivalent of the earth rotating around the sun, Eric broke eye contact, released my arms, and stepped back. "Couldn't bear having to arrest you for interfering with a police investigation," he said in a gruff voice. "But if I find you snooping around Marcus's property, I will."

With my heart pogoing around in my chest, I held up the curled fingers of my right hand, the smallest one extended. "I solemnly pinky swear not to snoop anywhere near Marcus Hall."

The look Eric sent me was half-filled with suspicion and half with the satisfaction of believing I saw him as enough of an authority figure to scare me back onto the straight and narrow.

Dimples followed by a genuine smile, he hooked his pinky finger with mine, and we shook on it. My toes curled inside my boots at that smile.

And one of them *might* have crossed over the other.

IF YOU DON'T LIKE the weather in Cape Discovery, just wait a minute. A common local adage, it once again proved true by late that afternoon. And as the rain clouds headed south, the warm autumn sun made quick work of drying the puddles on the sidewalks. I still had April's phone number from when I'd called her earlier in the year, but this time, my call went straight to voicemail. Next, I tried Birdie's, but she informed me April had moved home first thing this morning.

Despite the detective's warning to keep away from his prime suspect, he'd said nothing about me dropping in on a minor one. So, as was my prerogative, I closed the store fifteen minutes early, and after promising Harry I'd return with a special treat of fish and chips for dinner, I drove to April's.

Much like the woman herself, April's house hid from casual passers-by down a private driveway. I knocked on her door, half expecting the lights inside to flick off—the old introverts' trick of pretending not to be home in order to avoid people.

However, she opened the door, resignation written on her face. "What now, Tessa?"

"Davy Jones." It was all I needed to say to receive a

Shakespearean sigh and a gesture for me to follow her inside.

Cardboard boxes lined the hallway, some already sealed with packing tape, others partially filled with stacks of books, DVDs, and mysterious objects wrapped in newspaper.

"You're moving?"

"Gave the landlord my notice yesterday. I've got a job interview in Christchurch next week."

I followed April into a bright, airy kitchen. Heat pumped out from an old-style wood-burning stove, and beneath it, a small terrier-like dog lay on its back. Four paws pointing to the ceiling, it snored the sleep of the drugged by heat exhaustion.

She didn't offer me a seat, but I sat at her kitchen table anyway, and she returned to chopping some strong-smelling leaves on the counter.

"Rosie told you," she said.

"Was it Alastair you were with that night?"

"With. Ditched. Embarrassed by. Take your pick. And yes, I bent the truth when you asked if I knew him. I really didn't *know* him at all."

"Did he ever explain why he left so suddenly?"

April blew a raspberry. "I never saw or spoke to him again after that evening. What kind of man ducks out on a woman *he* asked on a date?" She scraped a palmful of leaves into a waiting bowl. "I'd caught him staring at me in the Daily Grind a few times, but it still took him three weeks of covert glances to work up the courage to say hello. He attempted to ask me out at least half a dozen times before he finally succeeded. And I only agreed to go because, well"—she lifted a shoulder and grabbed another bunch of leaves from the basket beside her—"I vaguely remembered him from high school and thought I'd take a walk down memory lane. Hey, it seemed better than spending Valentine's Day alone again. Ha. So much for that."

"Alastair humiliated you in front of everyone in that restaurant," I said. "No one would blame you for hunting him down and kicking his butt to the curb." They might blame her for cracking his skull like a hard-boiled egg, though.

"He wasn't worth the effort. It's not as if I actually *cared* about him."

"Unlike your long-distance relationship? With that man you met online?"

Her cheeks flushed a dull red. "How do you know about that?"

"You mentioned you were in a long-distance relationship. How do most long-distance relationships start these days? Sign of the times."

"Yeah. How did we survive before the web connected us to the world?" She barked out a bitter sound of amusement. "I thought Chase and I had a *connection*—a real one."

"Tell me about him."

Like many a woman with a broken heart, she was only too happy to dish the dirt on the man who'd shattered it.

Reader's Digest condensed version:

April met Chase Parker through KiwiConnect—he'd reached out to her initially.

Chase worked in the Colorado Rocky Mountains as a national park ranger, and April's knowledge of edible plants and sustainable living fascinated him. As an added bonus, Chase was hella handsome and a good listener. All of their communication occurred via chat rooms and email.

Chase wanted to immigrate to New Zealand and marry

her, but the health of his widowed mother, who'd raised him on her own, was a major hindrance.

April had regularly transferred sums of money into his bank account to help with medical bills and the cost of moving him and his mother, plus shipping all their worldly possessions.

Then one day, he'd mentioned something in passing about a particular plant growing in the Rocky Mountains that any ranger worth his salt wouldn't get wrong, and April had finally gotten suspicious.

She'd dug a little deeper into their exchanges and soon realized one could have driven a snowplow through some of the holes in Chase's story. Refusing to contribute another thousand dollars toward his mom's bills—which seemed so plentiful it was a miracle the woman was still alive—she cut him off cold turkey.

Old Chase wasn't happy 'bout that.

By the time April reached the end of her story, her hands were shaking so much she had to put down the knife. Thankfully. Because I'd been getting kind of concerned that she might decide to go all stabby on the messenger. So to speak.

"Thanks to my insecurities, I played right into his scam. Used up a fair chunk of my savings in the process." Folding her lips over her braces, she slanted me a glance, tears making her eyes shiny and red-rimmed. "What a gullible sap I was. Personally, I blame the movie industry and Jane Austen."

"Sorry that happened to you." I wouldn't patronize by telling her there were plenty more fish in the sea and wouldn't belittle her pain by sharing my own experiences of gullibility and rejection.

"Thanks." She sniffed and transferred the next batch of

chopped herbs to her bowl. "Anyway, I'm sure you didn't visit just to listen to me whine about being a fool, so why are you here?"

"Um." *Think, Tessa, think!* "I wanted to ask if you might be willing to come to one of our Crafting for Calmness classes and talk to us about the medicinal properties of herbs and plants growing locally. But since you're moving..."

"Oh!" April's face brightened. "I'm sure I could fit you in before I go."

While she thought out loud, planning the plants she could talk about, I nodded in what I hoped were the right places while pondering what my real intention had been for coming here.

It boiled down to wanting to judge for myself whether she could afford to pay her runaway date to shoot Dominic. If she was telling the truth about her online scammer, possibly not. Although not an exorbitant sum, ten thousand dollars wasn't exactly chump change to most people.

As for her cold-bloodedly murdering Alastair? I wasn't so confident of her innocence there. Maybe her runaway date's reappearance had been a trigger ready to pull after 'Chase' made a fool of her. But was April's con man in any way relevant to the Dominic-Alastair-Marcus mystery?

Or just another empty rabbit hole my mind wanted to dive into?

FOURTEEN

"Honest to Betsy," exclaimed Beth Chadwick, one of tonight's volunteers at the beginners class, "what did people expect the Pavlova bigwigs to do after such scandal?"

Nods of agreement ran around Unraveled's worktable, punctuated by the soft clack of knitting needles. Pavlova Productions washing their hands of Cape Discovery as a potential location was tonight's hottest goss topic. Apparently, two murders and a killer, or killers, running around un-arrested wasn't the kind of publicity the movie people wanted any part of.

"Money is always the bottom line." Mum pointed to a dropped stitch of the woman next to her before continuing, "But let's not forget that two people are dead."

No one had forgotten, and so the conversation veered into speculation over Marcus's involvement.

Mum rolled her eyes at me, and I sent her a wry smile. You'd have more chance of knitting spider-silk into a scarf than stopping Discovery locals from gossiping.

One of the beginners was approaching the end of her ball

of yarn, so Mum volunteered to fetch another and teach her how to join it. I hadn't had time to speak to her alone all evening, so I followed her into the store. While she ran a fingertip down the worsted-weight yarn, searching for the correct shade, I leaned nonchalantly against the shelf next to her.

She gave me a querying eyebrow with coordinating, "Hmm?"

I didn't know how to put all the thoughts racing around my head into words. Oliver, Eric, Birdie, Cora, April, Dominic, Alastair, Marcus—so many loose ends tying themselves into knots in my brain. And I had no clue how to untangle them.

Guess my struggle must've registered on my face, as Mum dropped the yarn she'd selected and pulled me into a hug. "I can hear you overthinking, sweetie," she said, rubbing my shoulder. "How about you choose one thought, no matter how random, and tell me?"

I sucked in a deep breath and plucked at one of those threads. "April Bradford and Marcus Hall both used an online dating site called KiwiConnect. Do you think that means anything?"

Mum's hand stilled on my shoulder, and she arched back to meet my gaze. "Other than they're lonely and money can't buy you happiness?"

"Did I hear you say KiwiConnect and Marcus Hall in the same breath?" Beth piped up from behind me.

I turned to see a carnivorous smile as she all but vibrated with the excitement of containing a juicy nugget of information. We all knew withholding gossip wasn't Beth's strong suit, so all I had to do was rearrange my features into an *I'm listening* face.

"I could tell you a story about Marcus Hall's venture

into online dating that'd make your hair curl," she said smugly. "Though I'm not one to talk out of turn."

Yeah, right. However, if it required a sacrifice to make her feel comfortable about blabbing, I'd happily provide it.

"I'm thinking of signing Sean up," I said. "It's about time he found a nice girl to settle down with. So if you have a cautionary tale about KiwiConnect, Beth, we're all ears."

Didn't need to look at Mum to know her jaw hit the floor, but before she could leap to defend her precious son's reputation, I subtly elbowed her arm and heard her teeth click together.

"Gosh," Beth said. "There's plenty of nice girls in Cape Discovery he could choose from without dredging through the desperate women using those dating sites." She gave an exaggerated shudder. "While Marcus isn't my favorite person by any stretch of the imagination, I do feel a teeny bit sorry for him."

"I think you'd better tell us what you know, Beth," my mum said.

Beth wrapped a bony hand around my wrist and tugged me over to the armchairs. With an air of authority, she sank into one and leaned toward me. "Well, as it happens, I'm good friends with Marcus's sister, Raelene. Earlier in the year, she confided to me that her brother had met a woman through KiwiConnect—a single mother in Thailand, no less."

Spidery tickles scurried over my scalp. "Go on."

"Oh yes. Apparently, Marcus was completely smitten with her. Raelene said she'd seen the woman's photo, and she was a real looker."

"Let me guess, this woman had a child?" Mum asked.

"An eight-year-old girl." Beth's lips twisted. "Afflicted with cerebral palsy, poor baby." She sniffed. "Whether she was any more real than her supposed mother, I couldn't tell you. But Marcus believed it and had been sending them money." Beth dipped her chin and raised her eyebrows. "Quite a bit of money over a number of months, according to Raelene. She warned her brother it could be a scam, but he wouldn't hear a word of it. This woman said as soon as her daughter was well enough to travel, they'd join Marcus in New Zealand."

Do I believe in coincidences? Sure. To a point. But this story smelled so fishy it stank up the room like Beth's famous tuna casserole left out in the sun. "What happened next?"

Beth sat back in her chair and lifted a nonchalant shoulder. "I'm afraid I don't know much more. Raelene said she asked her brother about this woman a few weeks ago, and he gave her a very curt reply. They were no longer dating. We both suspected he'd found out his Thai lotus was, in fact, a computer nerd living in his parents' basement and making a nice little income out of duping gullible, lonely people."

The spidery tickles now zoomed up and down my spine.

"How much money does Raelene think her brother sent this woman?" I asked.

Beth checked over her shoulder before lowering her voice. "Hundreds of dollars, perhaps even thousands." She made a clicking sound with her tongue. "I don't know which would've upset Marcus more—the hit to his bank account or the hit to his pride at having been made a fool of."

Ice replaced the tickles, creeping into every crevice and freezing me to the spot.

Was that the connection between April, Marcus, Dominic, and the missing laptop?

Had Dominic been the computer nerd in Beth's scenario?

THE FOLLOWING MORNING, I baked a couple of salmon and asparagus quiches. At lunchtime, I cut into one for Harry and took the other with me to deliver to Birdie. Yes, I had hidden agenda for hand-delivering food and a small bouquet from Bloomin' Great Discovery next door.

One, I wanted to check Birdie was doing okay, knowing that the man suspected of murdering her nephew lived just over the next ridge.

And two, I wanted to find out just how tech-savvy said nephew had been.

There was no sign of Cora's car when I pulled up in front of Birdie's house, and I'll admit to some small amount of relief that I wouldn't have to deal with her. I collected the quiche and the makings of a garden salad and walked up to the front door. No one answered my knock, but I decided to check out back in case Birdie was pottering in her herb garden and hadn't heard me. Basket over my arm, I strolled around her house.

And spotted Marcus trying to vamoose across the backyard, a tool of some kind clutched in his hand.

"Hey!" Of their own accord, my feet moved faster, bell peppers and tomatoes and peppery radishes rolling around in my basket. "Where are you going? Hey, *Marcus*." I raised my voice to an unattractive holler, using his name so he knew I recognized him.

Dude, you are so busted.

And Marcus seemed to realize it, his rolling gait slowing

to a cocky saunter as he shoved whatever he'd held in his hand into the waistband of his pants.

"Ah, Tessa. Didn't hear you drive up." He planted his gumboot-clad feet wide and folded his arms across his chest.

As if he had every right to be on MacKenzie land, regardless of the fact he was suspected of a double homicide.

"I'm not surprised."

That my mama hadn't raised an idiot ensured I kept a healthy distance from Marcus. Mentally calculating the weight of the basket and with spatial awareness of how wide I could swing it in an arc toward his head—should the need arise—I sent a pointed stare at his crotch. Outlined under the grubby denim of his jeans was a narrow wedge topped with a bright yellow plastic handle. "Have I just caught you about to add breaking and entering to your long list of vices?"

While Marcus sputtered about paying his poor bereaved neighbor a neighborly visit, I sneaked a quick glance over my shoulder to Birdie's back door. It appeared he'd been unsuccessful in gaining entry before I disturbed him. I waved my free hand to get his attention. "How about we skip your empty excuses and my correct assumption you were up to no good and get to the part where you tell me what you're looking for? Or should I call the cops?"

As backup to my threat, I dug my phone out of my pocket and tapped the screen as if partially activating the emergency number. Glancing down, I noticed I'd accidentally opened the camera app and managed to take a blast of photos of my foot.

Marcus glared at me but darted worried glances at my phone. "Fine. I saw Birdie and that Cora woman leave with a bunch of shopping bags. Thought I might poke around her house while they were out, to see what I could see."

I must've looked unconvinced or irritated by his lack of candor or perhaps a mixture of both because Marcus unfolded his arms, planted hands on hips and blew out a long sigh, his eyes downcast. "I was hoping to find something to prove I had nothing to do with that young man's death."

"You mean your former employee, Alastair Brown?"

"He was a mixed-up kid who trusted the wrong people."

Like you? I couldn't help but wonder. Yet I thought I detected an honest note of regret in his voice.

"A mixed-up kid who may have shot and killed a man you clearly hated."

"Dominic MacKenzie was rotten to the core. Have you learned nothing about what sort of man he was, girlie?" he sneered. "Why, I wouldn't be at all surprised if he'd convinced Alastair to become his partner in some nefarious scam and it fatally backfired on him—pun intended."

An accusation that made no sense to me—except for the scam part.

What did a park ranger with a sick mother in the US and a solo mother with a sick daughter in Thailand have in common?

"A scam involving your online Thai girlfriend?" Though I suspected Marcus's solo mother and April's park ranger were one and the same person toying with them.

Via a computer screen.

Marcus recoiled, his expression that of a man who'd stuck his hand through the bars of the cage to pet a fluffy, Disney-eyed creature only to have said creature chomp into his finger with razor-sharp teeth. "How did you know about her?"

"*Have you learned nothing* about small-town gossip?"

"I pay no attention to gossipmongers," he said piously.

"Well, maybe you should. Might have saved you some heartache, embarrassment, and getting caught up in a murder investigation."

Marcus studied me for a long moment. I recognized that look on his face; I'd seen it a million times on the high school kids I'd counseled. It was an expression that told me the wearer needed to unburden themselves.

With a huff of resignation, Marcus scrubbed a hand down his face. I took advantage of this by activating the recording app on my phone but made sure he only saw me tuck it back into my pocket.

"This woman reached out to you first?" I asked.

"Lily said I had kind eyes and an honest face." He snorted, shaking his head. "And like an old fool, I lapped it up. There's something to be said for that adage 'if it sounds too good to be true, it probably is.' Should've twigged something was up when she mentioned how expensive her daughter's medical bills were."

"When did she first ask you for money?"

"Oh, she didn't ask. She was much too smart for that. It was about two weeks after we started chatting online that she brought up the subject of her sick daughter. But when I offered to help financially, she refused, saying she was too proud to take my money. We went back and forth over a number of emails until she eventually agreed to borrow a small amount, just to tide them over. The next time she mentioned having to work extra hours in her job as a beautician, she was less vehement in her objection to me sending her money."

Without interrupting, I allowed Marcus to lay out and dissect their one-sided passionate love affair. Until he reached the part about his most significant financial donation: a combination of paying outstanding medical bills and enough money for Lily to leave Bangkok with her daughter and become his fiancée.

Except one drama after another required more and more deposits into her bank account.

"Nothing in your correspondence raised a red flag?"

It seemed unimaginable that a man who appeared quite pragmatic had been suckered in so completely.

"There were plenty of red flags, but I chose to ignore them," he admitted. "I believed I was in love, and love can make you stupid."

"So when did you wise up?"

"The moment of clarity came when I called into the Daily Grind to pick up an order for my sister. Dominic was sitting at a table, hammering away on his laptop with his back to me. I found myself watching him work, watching him jab one key over and over as if it kept sticking. Let me tell you, my blood ran cold when I noticed it was the 'q' key he was punching."

"Why was the 'q' key significant?"

"Lily started missing q's in her emails and messages, and we joked about her 'minding her p's and q's.' She told me her laptop was well past its use-by date, so I'd planned to surprise her with a new one."

"Then you noticed Dominic hitting his 'q' key and put two and two together." I imagined the shock, disbelief, then fury as it dawned on Marcus he'd been played. And played by a man he'd already disliked on the principle that he had control over land Marcus coveted.

Marcus's hands flexed and bunched at his sides. "It's

crazy the weird stuff you think about when you find out everything you thought you knew is a lie." He gave a bitter chuckle. "All I could think about while I paid for Raelene's order was the gall of Dominic, doing his dirty work on a cruddy, outdated computer after all the money I'd sent him."

"The computer you hoped to find inside Birdie's house?" I asked.

He glared at me. "There's confidential information on that laptop, I'm sure of it."

The sound of a car engine purring up the driveway reached our ears, and Marcus reacted like someone had poked him with a cattle prod. He lurched away from me and broke into a shambling run, no doubt cutting through the orchard to his land the way Alastair Brown had.

I could only hope that one of the alpacas would object and—totally out of character—decide to bite him.

As I walked around the house to meet Birdie and Cora, I thought about this mysterious laptop both Marcus and April seemed keen to get their hands on. And the phone and tablet Alastair might well have taken with him after killing Dominic. Had that been the amateur hitman's goal right from the get-go? Murder MacKenzie for payback and greed while also confiscating any evidence of Marcus's more personal motive?

Except there can't have been any evidence on Dominic's other devices, otherwise Marcus wouldn't have risked a break-in attempt to locate his enemy's laptop.

So where on earth was it?

FIFTEEN

When a brother offers to treat her to lunch, an older and wiser sister has every right to be both flattered and suspicious.

As it turned out, suspicion was the correct response.

I balked when Sean told me where we were eating. "Really, Sean?"

He gave me his most endearing innocent smile. "What? We're all grownups, aren't we? Besides, the Stone does a great loaded fries. Extra bacon and cheese, just the way you like it."

"You're about as subtle as a steamroller," I muttered.

But I followed him into the pub.

Sean was pulling out all the stops. Then again, my brother could charm a tui out of a nectar feast with a mere smile, so I shouldn't see him railroading me into a meal in enemy territory as a failing on my part.

Not that Oliver was the enemy.

It was just, for want of a more original word, awkward.

We found a table and gave Lucinda our order, and I

offered up humble thanks to the universe for the lack of a certain bar owner working alongside his staff.

"So," Sean said once he'd returned from the bar with a beer for himself and a lemonade for me—I intended to keep my wits about me while there was even the slightest chance of embarrassing myself in Oliver's pub. "How's it going with…?" He tipped his head toward the far end of the bar and the office behind it.

Gee whiskers. That was scarily direct. It didn't take a rocket scientist to figure out who was bankrolling this impromptu lunch.

"Are you asking for yourself? If so, it's kinda creepy that you're taking a sudden interest in my personal life." I couldn't bring myself to say S.E.X life out loud when there were occupied tables nearby. "Or are you asking for Mum? Which is also creepy plus a little pathetic that you've stooped to becoming her spy."

Sean's eyes bugged wide. "Jeez, Tess. I was just checking if you were okay after Saturday afternoon."

"Perfectly okay. Peachy keen. Box of birds, in fact." For some reason, whenever I lied to my family, I resorted to the vocabulary of my grandparents' generation.

Fixing my lips into some semblance of a cheery smile, I double-checked over my shoulder before mimicking my brother's head-tip toward the office. "We're just friends." Then, in a fit of inspiration, I added, "Like your mate Gavin's friends with April."

"Uh-huh." Sean rocked back on his chair legs and folded his arms. "First of all, Gavin and April are just friends because she doesn't know how much he's into her. And secondly—"

I jerked forward, my glass of lemonade rattling on the

tabletop. "Wait! Forget secondly. Gavin's into April? As in, he *likes* her, likes her?"

Sean rolled his eyes. "Now who has all the emotional maturity of a thirteen-year-old?" At my glare, he shrugged. "Yeah, he likes her, likes her. He has done for years. Never had the guts to do anything about it, though."

"And she's unaware of this?"

"Don't ask me. You're the one who went away to university to get a fancy degree in figuring people out."

The casual way my brother dug up a bone of contention that had moldered underground in my family's collective memory didn't make it sting any less. My ambitious mother seemed the only one in my family who'd understood my need to leave Cape Discovery for university. While Dad and my grandparents had been supportive, I knew they'd hoped I'd choose to study and then work closer to them. As for my siblings, my eldest sister, Jill, believed I'd set out to prove I was smarter than the rest of the Wakefield kids, and middle sister, Kelly, was too consumed by her own desire to create the ultimate white-picket-fence family. And Sean? Well, I hadn't thought Sean cared either way what I did.

Guess I'd been wrong about that.

Alert the media! Tessa Wakefield had been wrong about something.

"And yet, your mind remains a mystery to me, little brother," I teased, hoping I'd successfully extracted any hurt from my tone. Sean hadn't exactly been a baby when I trundled off to university. "What there is of it."

That earned me another eye-roll as he dropped his chair back onto four legs and reached for his beer. My brother studied me over the bottle. "You really hadn't figured out that Gavin has a thing for April?"

I tried to recall any occasions I'd seen them in close

proximity and whether I'd witnessed what I perceive to be the normal indications of interest. Frequent glances and lingering looks. Flirty banter. Accidental-on-purpose touching. Couldn't say I'd noticed any of these, but I could check all three off my list when it came to my interactions with Oliver.

And Detective Mana.

Huh. Just goes to show I have no idea what the heck I'm talking about.

"Nope. Must've escaped my hawk-like attention."

Sean made a *pfft* sound as a plate of loaded fries appeared over my shoulder. "What escaped your hawk-like attention?" asked a very male, very sexy, very Oliver-ish voice as the greasy, salty deliciousness was placed in front of me.

Ignoring bacon's siren call, I kept my expression neutral as Oliver walked around me to deliver Sean's order. He wore his usual uniform of denim and plaid, with the addition of a black server apron slung low around his hips. It said more about me than him that I found an apron as sexy as a gunslinger's holster.

I cleared my throat while giving him what I hoped was an imperious stare. "My brother was just telling me in our *private conversation* that Gavin isn't as far into the mutual-friend zone with April Bradford as she thinks he is."

From his apron pocket, Oliver produced flatware wrapped in a paper napkin and offered it to me. My fingers brushed his as I took the knife-and-fork duo, and against all reason, my stomach did handsprings. One of us hadn't put the other anywhere near the friend zone either.

"Is that right?" He didn't seem at all perturbed at being called out for eavesdropping. Quite possibly because they considered eavesdropping a competitive sport in Cape Discovery.

"I'm not sure if that's true, though." Or if it was important for any reason other than even April's S.E.X life looking more optimistic than mine. "Did you notice anything that evening they were here together?"

Oliver dropped Sean's flatware on the table beside his fries—with extra *extra* bacon and cheese. "Can't say I paid much attention to who had the hots for whom. But Gavin was pretty quick to jump to April's defense when she started getting into it with the Pavlova guys." His lips twisted. "Come to think of it, Gavin was looking at her the way Maki looks at a lamb shank bone."

"Hungrily?" I supplied.

"Maki's not that straightforward when it comes to bones. First, he eyes it up warily as if it's too good to be true. Then he sniffs it and watches the giver, trying to work out whether it's gonna be snatched away. Once he gets a taste of it, he's all territorial warning growls. And finally, once he's comfortable knowing the bone is his, he's cutely protective of it and will drag it around for days, hiding it in different spots."

"And this relates to April how? She's hardly a bone."

He chuckled. "No. But maybe in Gavin's mind, she's a prize worth fighting for."

Sean picked up a fry dripping with gooey cheese. "Gav fight? Nah. A puff of wind could blow him over. The only thing I reckon he'd get his hands dirty for is for one of his causes—and even then, he'd rather organize a protest or post flyers around town."

"Well, there you go. He's a lover, not a fighter." Oliver's smile, taut with something dark lurking beneath the surface, sent another shiver racing down my spine. "Can I get you anything else?"

I shook my head then watched as he walked away. And, *great hairy yarn balls*, the man truly was a reversible hottie—equally as yummy from the back as from the front.

But his last comment about Gavin made me wonder. Was Oliver a lover or a fighter?

Oliver braced his palms on the bar, muscles bunching underneath his flannel shirtsleeves as he murmured something to Lucinda. Perhaps Oliver Novak was both because it didn't take much to visualize him with bloody knuckles after pummeling a man who'd dared to besmirch the honor of the woman he loved.

And perhaps it was time I tossed the stash of dog-eared romantic paperbacks hidden in my closet.

AFTER LUNCH WITH MY BROTHER, I struggled to settle back into my happy place of discussing the virtues of our latest range of locally spun alpaca yarn. Harry, bless him, told me to go walk off whatever excess energy was making me buzz around like a wasp caught in a mason jar.

Letting my feet guide me—often a terrible idea—I found myself on Pirates' Way. I'd poked at Sean about his drinking buddy until, irritated, he'd told me to talk to Mrs. Schmidt if I wanted her son's life story.

So that's where my wild-goose-chasing feet took me. To the end of Pirates' Way and a neat bungalow with a yellow-and-black striped letterbox out front. A sign advertising 'Fresh Honey for Sale' swung from it, and I remembered seeing the same honeybee logo on an awning at the farmers market.

That gave me as good an excuse as any to pay Mrs. Schmidt a visit. Harry was rather partial to honey smeared thickly on his toast or stirred into his tea.

As I strolled down the driveway, I spotted another sign pointing toward the backyard. Next to the garage, shelves filled with labeled jars of honey lined a small lean-to. In the shade of the lean-to, Mrs. Schmidt sat snoozing on a deck chair, her hands laced over her belly, which was covered in—you guessed it—honeybee-print coveralls.

My footsteps gritting on the broken-shell driveway must have alerted her, as her eyes sprang open. "Gav? You're home early. Oh..." She spotted me. "Sorry! I must've dozed off. You're one of Alan and Maggie's girls, aren't you?"

I smiled. "Tessa. My brother, Sean, and your son are mates."

"That's right. They were in chess club together at high school, I believe. Gav does love his chess."

This was news to me—considering I could beat Sean at checkers with one hand tied behind my back, I suspected there must be a girl involved in this unlikely equation. I'd need to fish for the information.

"Do Gavin and Sean hang out with any of their other school friends? Was April Bradford at Cape Discovery High with them?"

"Believe she was now that you mention it. She and that foster boy from down the road used to follow Gav around like shadows." Mrs. Schmidt flashed a proud smile. "Those kids used to get bullied something terrible until my boy stuck up for them and put those nasty bullies in their place. After that, they both worshiped the ground he walked on."

"April had a crush on Gavin?"

Mrs. Schmidt waved her hand as if brushing aside one of her bees. "Puppy love. She grew out of it." Frown lines appeared between her eyebrows. "Funny the way things work out. My boy loves championing the underdog—it's his default setting, you know—but he had no interest in that young lady back then. She was a couple of years younger, with pimples and buckteeth. The bullies had a field day with her. Now..." She chuckled and slapped a palm on her thigh. "Now she's grown into a right pretty lass. He's sweet on her, I think, but she's having none of it."

Alert the media a second time. It appeared my brother was actually right.

Then I remembered something Constable Austin had said about Alastair being a foster kid, and on a hunch, I asked, "The boy from down the road that Gavin protected at school, do you remember his name?"

"Oh, dear, yes." As Mrs. Schmidt's eyes grew shiny, she produced an old-fashioned hankie from the pocket of her coveralls and dabbed her nose. "Poor lad, I recognized his name from that newspaper. Alastair Brown. He was quite a few years younger than my Gav, and the kids used to tease him mercilessly about his red hair and freckles. I often wondered what happened to that boy, and now I know." She made a clicking noise with her tongue. "A life of crime. Such a waste."

"Gavin didn't mention that Alastair had, um, passed away unexpectedly?"

Mrs. Schmidt shook her head. "Didn't want to upset me. Always looking out for the people he loves, that's my Gavin. He takes good care of the old folks at Sunnyville."

"I saw him up there on the weekend. He seemed very good with them." But I'd heard enough about Saint Gavin. "Did April know Alastair?"

At Mrs. Schmidt's bemused frown, I added, "I mean,

when they were younger. You said they followed Gavin around. Did the three of them become close mates?"

"Wouldn't say they were that friendly. You know how kids are—all about appearances. Gavin had mates his own age, like your brother. I always used to see April with her nose in a book at the public library. Alastair, golly, he was a weedy kid on a bike last time I saw him. His foster family moved out of the area before he finished high school." Her expression brightened. "Oh, there was that summer reading club the library sponsored years ago. I remember seeing the two of them sitting side by side at a table, whispering over their stack of books. Perhaps they were friends. They were both outcasts in their own way, so it was nice they could bond over it."

Fancy that, as Nana Dee-Dee would've said.

Mrs. Schmidt heaved herself to her feet. "Listen to me, gas-bagging the day away. How many jars would you like?"

While she selected two jars from the shelf and I dug out my wallet, I couldn't help but wonder how long that childhood bond between April and Alastair had lasted.

Into adulthood? Likely. Although April hadn't mentioned knowing Alastair when he was a boy targeted by bullies because of his red hair. To give her the benefit of the doubt, perhaps she hadn't recognized him. At first.

But surely, at some stage during their Davy Jones dinner date, she'd figured it out? Perhaps heard about his prison time subsequently, and two years later, when she needed a handy criminal, convinced Alastair to get rid of the ultimate bully? The man who'd humiliated her and stolen her money.

Unfortunately, there was the pesky issue of April being seen at the Stone's Throw on the night Alastair died.

Unless... Could she have sneaked out and followed

Alastair's car to the rest area? Timing-wise, she could've returned to her group's table in less than an hour with the plausible excuse of a bathroom break and chatting with other friends in the crowded and busy bar. Alastair wouldn't have seen her as a threat if she'd slid into the passenger seat next to him at the rest area. She could've arranged the fake evidence to shift the suspicion onto Marcus, and with a bit of effort and the assistance of a sloped parking lot, given Alastair's vehicle a push toward the river, letting momentum do the rest.

Possible. Scarily possible.

However, would she have had the cast-iron stomach and ruthlessness required to kill him?

That, I didn't know.

And not even Mrs. Schmidt's sample of honeycomb melting on my tongue could remove the acrid taste of revulsion from my mouth.

SIXTEEN

Since Cora would 'sooner poke an eye out with a knitting needle than use one,' according to Birdie, I once again picked her up so she could attend Thursday evening's Crafting for Calmness. She was almost unrecognizable as the woman who'd walked into Unraveled's workroom a week ago. There was—and I hate to sound clichéd—a spring in her step and a sparkle in her eye as she greeted everyone.

While I was pleased to see Nana Dee-Dee's old friend enjoying herself, my mind couldn't stop spinning its wheels. Should I or shouldn't I reach out to Eric with what I'd learned about April? Prior to the class, I'd wasted an inordinate amount of time staring at my phone's messaging icon. Until—no closer to a decision—I switched to autopilot and got through the session by knitting and purling my way to distraction.

On the drive back, I listened with only half an ear as Birdie shared details of the plans she and Cora had put in motion. Most of these plans involved Cora moving into the farmhouse with Birdie. Cora would help out with the administrative aspects of the Clowder Motel and the animal rescue until her baby was born, then take on more physical jobs around the orchard while Birdie provided daycare for her step-great-grandchild.

"But, Birdie, how sure are you that Cora is who she says she is?"

She chuckled. "I may be old, but I'm a MacKenzie through and through. First thing Monday morning, I called my lawyer and then sent off for a DNA kit."

"Oh." I shot her a sheepish grin as I steered my car along her driveway. "I shouldn't have doubted you could take care of yourself." We rounded the last curve, and her brightly lit house came into view with Cora's car parked outside of it. "It'll be nice for you, having company and a new baby to fuss over."

"Exactly. I know Cora seems as prickly as a sea urchin, but if you gave her a chance, I think the two of you could become friends. Why don't you come in for a cuppa and a chat?"

"Tempting and all as that sounds"—as tempting as trying to swallow said sea urchin—"think I'll take a rain check."

She patted my hand. "You do look a bit peaked, honeybunch. Another time then."

Once we'd said our goodbyes, I waited until Birdie reached Cora, who stood just inside the open front door, before turning my car in the direction of home. But as I puttered down the driveway, my foot eased on the brake when I drew alongside the cutting through the trees—the cutting that led to the kitty litter dumping ground.

A question popped into my head: *Where's the best place to hide something you don't want anyone to find?*

Followed by the 'keep it simple, stupid' answer: *In a place that no one in their right mind would want to look.*

Like the women who stashed money or candy in a tampon box, where they knew the men in their lives would never check. Or a man who ran a catfishing scam right under the noses of the community he lived in.

April had already searched the cattery itself, but had she thought to dig around in Dominic's litter-recycling area?

Figuring that question would bug me in the middle of the night, I stopped my car and, armed with the mini emergency flashlight from the glove compartment, hopped out, leaving the keys in the ignition. Just a quick poke around, and I'd be on my way. Without the car's headlights lighting the way, it was as dark among the trees as my kitties' furry coats, and despite the starry sky twinkling overhead, starlight alone wasn't enough to guide me along the cleared path to Dominic's shed.

Thank goodness for Harry's insistence that I stock my car with a first aid kit and flashlight. Obviously, my granddad knew the kinds of predicaments I was likely to land in.

As leaves rustled all around, from overhead came the distinctive two-tone call of the small owl that, in Māori tradition, was seen as a watchful guardian and sometimes the bearer of bad news. My hope was that its soft *more-pork...more-pork* cry meant it would swoop down and save me from any unwanted insects dropping on my head from above.

After tripping over numerous roots on the rough path, I finally burst into the clearing. I headed straight for the first mound of untreated kitty litter and, flashlight clenched between my teeth, picked up a nearby shovel and deconstructed the pile.

Nothing but poo and litter pellets.

Ditto with the second pile.

Sure, I *could* have gotten down on hands and knees to comb through it just to be sure, but there were limits to what I was prepared to do. Instead, I shone the flashlight toward the shed and the trays of cleaned, drying litter. Now, that would make more sense.

Leaving the shovel where it was, I strode into the shed and sifted my fingers through the first tray—making a mental note to use up my travel-sized bottle of hand sanitizer back in the car as soon as I was done. First tray was a bust, but on the second...my fingers scraped over something with a hard edge. Litter flying left and right, I uncovered an ancient-looking laptop wrapped in heavy-duty clear plastic.

Bingo.

I unfolded the plastic from around my prize and opened the laptop's lid. Quickly, before the law-abiding section of my brain could object, I hit the 'on' button. Bless Dominic's cotton socks, the dearly departed hadn't bothered using password protection, leaving his computer immediately accessible. Like pretty maids all in a row, folder icons lined up across the screen. Amongst the dozen or so names I didn't recognize, there were two I did—April Bradford and Marcus Hall. I selected the one with April's name.

Bathed in the screen's glow, I clicked on the folder and winced as I scanned its contents. Copies of email correspondence between April and 'Chase,' together with records of the large sums of money April had transferred to Chase—aka Dominic MacKenzie. That 'Chase' and Birdie's nephew were the same person was painfully obvious. And from the last email in the list—with a subject line of 'Give back my money sleazeball or YOU'RE DEAD!'—no wonder she'd been desperate to get her hands on the missing laptop.

As the mouse arrow hovered over the email, ready to click, a surreptitious scuff came from behind me. My scalp itching with icy pinpricks, I spun, the flashlight beam skittering off the shed's walls to the open doorway.

And the person caught midstep in its light.

"APRIL?" The name circling my head and momentarily trapped in my throat exploded on a whoosh of air.

But the looming shape blocking my only exit wasn't April.

Not even close.

Not the right height; this person's head nearly reached the top of the doorframe. And not the right gender, highlighted by my flashlight beam as it crept upward from hairy legs encased in cargo shorts to the frown that told me Gavin Schmidt wasn't about to invite me for tea and cookies.

"What are you doing here?"

A dumb question, I'll admit. But surely I could be forgiven for asking it, as he wasn't who I'd expected to gatecrash my laptop-finding expedition.

"I've been following you. Mum said you'd stopped by this afternoon, asking about me." He raised a hand in front of his face. "Will you stop shining that light in my face? It's blinding me."

"Sorry." I repositioned the flashlight beam, aiming it at his midsection. "I was asking your mum about *April*. She mentioned that you used to hang out with her and Alastair."

"What of it?"

"They must've looked up to you as their hero."

"I rescued them from a pack of bullies a few times. Someone had to look out for them."

How else had Gavin looked out for the girl he'd developed feelings for? The middle pieces of this complicated jigsaw puzzle were slowly falling into place.

"But you continued to look out for April after that, didn't you?"

"She's a good person who's never hurt a soul."

"So when she confided in you that the park ranger she'd had an online relationship with was actually Dominic catfishing her, as her friend, you were furious on her behalf."

"Yeah, I was. Anyone would be. He took her money then broke her heart."

"Which you wanted for yourself because you were also in love with her."

He remained silent, but I noted the slight slump of his shoulders.

"April confronted Dominic," I said, "but she had no proof. That's where you stepped in to be her hero again."

"I thought if I could get the proof for her, she might see me as more than some weak crusader who was all talk and no action."

"The proof being this laptop?"

"I called Alastair, assuming he'd probably be on friendly terms with some dubious characters after spending time in prison. When I asked if he knew anyone who'd remove a laptop from the owner's possession, he said he'd do it."

"Alastair offered to break in and steal it?"

"It was no big deal. He'd done it before, and he felt like he owed me a favor. Alastair said he'd watch the MacKenzies for a few days, get to know their routine and be in and out, no problem. Course, he reported that both Dominic and his aunt were real homebodies and rarely left the property, so we decided he'd jimmy the back door one night after the old girl had gone to bed. He'd take a crowbar or something to threaten Dominic with—and demand he hand over his laptop."

"But he ended up with a loaded gun? Not to mention the small matter of ten thousand dollars in cash."

Gavin shrugged. "Turned out Marcus Hall contacted Alastair shortly after I had. He wanted Dominic's laptop too, plus he had the added incentive of the property he'd been after for years. Only Marcus offered Alastair a wad of cash to use a gun he'd provide to get rid of MacKenzie once and for all. But he had to do it the week following Easter, so Marcus had the airtight alibi of being in Auckland."

My flashlight beam must have revealed my shocked expression.

"Alastair wasn't a killer," he said. "He planned to get the laptop for me, get out, and use the ten grand to start a new life for himself in Aussie."

"What went wrong?"

"Dominic surprised him in the laundry, and the gun went off by accident. Gutshot, Alastair reckoned. He panicked and shot him again but kept his wits about him enough to grab Dominic's phone and tablet and hoof it through the orchard to Marcus's place, where he'd parked his car. The guy was almost hyperventilating when we met at our prearranged spot."

Not surprising, given that he'd just shot a man three times.

"Where he gave you Dominic's devices…"

"Totally useless, they were. Nothing but solitaire games and garden-variety porn." He shot me a sly look. "As soon as I found out what Alastair had done, I destroyed them both. I'm no idiot."

No. But it dawned on me that Marcus wasn't the only

one with blood on his hands—and in Gavin's case, Alastair's blood. Literally.

"Of course you aren't." I adjusted my tone of voice to soothing former-guidance-counselor mode. "And I'm sure April appreciates how you've gone to so much trouble to help her."

His mouth twisted. "I couldn't take *any* credit for helping her after Alastair screwed things up. Telling him to keep calm and lie low didn't work. He wanted to hand himself in to the cops. I couldn't let him do that, could I? He'd ruin everything."

A chill crept down my spine. "You arranged to meet him at the Stone's Throw on Saturday night."

"Heck no. In the graveyard across the road, but the fool came in for a drink and couldn't resist chatting up some chick."

I risked poking at a sore spot. "April wouldn't have been too pleased to see him again. Not after he humiliated her on their date."

Gavin inhaled sharply. "They went on a date? When?"

"A couple of years back. Alastair bailed on her when she went to the ladies' room."

"Why the little..." His hands clenched into fists at his sides.

"You caused a scene with the Pavlova crowd so people would remember you being there. Then you sneaked out and met up with Alastair."

"We took separate cars to the rest area, and I tried—genuinely tried—to convince him it was in both of our best interests for him to cut his losses in Cape Discovery and stick to his original plan of a one-way flight to Australia. I even attempted to sweeten the deal by offering another two grand in cash. Hard pass, he reckoned, then spouted some garbage about how he couldn't live with his conscience and turning over a new leaf. Alastair promised he wouldn't bring me into it when he fessed up to the cops, but as I said, I'm no idiot. He would've spilled his guts eventually. He left me no choice."

I swallowed a spit-less lump in my throat. Whatever Alastair had done, he'd planned to own up to it but had made the mistake of trusting his old protector, who truly hadn't had his best interests at heart.

"So you...?"

"Yeah." His *'nuff said* tone conveyed the rest of his sordid little story.

He'd murdered Alastair and done a reasonable job of pinning the whole thing on Marcus Hall. Marcus, who was still guilty of conspiring to kill his neighbor but was, at least, innocent of bludgeoning a man to death.

As Gavin folded his arms and leaned against the doorframe, my flashlight revealed the wiry strength in his arms. If physically capable of assisting elderly people in and out of wheelchairs, he was physically capable of putting me in one. Permanently. Or worse.

"And if you hadn't insisted on sticking your nose where it didn't belong, Marcus Hall would have got his just desserts. Now"—he angled his upper body forward menacingly—"I have another problem."

"Me?" I squeaked.

"You," he agreed.

I racked my brain for something to say to buy myself more time. Although not expecting the calvary or even my brave kitties to save the day this time, I just needed a moment to come up with a game plan.

"Actually, you have two problems," I blurted. "Did you know April's planning to move to Christchurch?"

I'd apologize to April later for a. suspecting her of murder, and b. throwing her under the bus with her psycho, wannabe boyfriend.

The edge of my flashlight beam caught the wide-open whites of his eyes and his slack jaw. "She's *what*?"

"Yep. Found her packing up her house on Tuesday afternoon."

"She never said a word—the ungrateful little..."

Tuning out his ranting list of unflattering adjectives, I zipped my gaze around the shed for a weapon. Searching for anything I could use to fight my way out of this shed. Unfortunately, I'd left the shovel outside, and the only thing close enough was the laptop—nope, wasn't about to risk damaging evidence—and...kitty litter.

Mohair-flecking kitty litter.

That was all I had, so that's what I'd use.

I scooped up a fistful and hurled it in Gavin's face—into his eyes, to be precise. With a yelp, he stumbled backward, and when his heel struck the raised doorstep, he fell out of the shed.

SEVENTEEN

Laptop jammed under my arm, I bolted outside, somehow managing to avoid Gavin's gangly limbs as he rolled around on the ground. Without pausing to check whether he'd bruised his tailbone, *highly likely*, or broken an ankle, *wishful thinking*, I raced toward the path. But at the last moment, I changed my mind and slipped around a bushy fern and into the undergrowth. Those long legs of his would carry him down the path much faster than I could run, so my best bet was to do as many small, frightened animals did when pursued by something bigger, meaner, and merciless.

Hide.

Low-lying branches, thorny bushes, and exposed roots attempted to thwart my progress as I clumsily pushed past. And from somewhere behind me, sticks cracking like gunfire underfoot marked Gavin's progress as he stumbled along in pursuit. With my flashlight acting as a beacon, I decided I'd take my chances and switched it off. Immediately, my toe connected with a root, and my teeth snapped down on my tongue. Blinking back tears, I hunkered down behind a tree, the taste of warm copper filling my mouth.

Boom, ba-da-boom, ba-da-boom. Blood pounding so loudly against my eardrums that I doubted I'd have heard a brass band passing nearby, I tucked myself into a tight ball and squeezed my eyes shut. Who needed boot camp to elevate your heart rate into the fat-burning zone when you could have a killer chase you through the woods?

Although my sense of direction was dubious at best, it sounded as if Kevin was moving away from me. A few hundred heartbeats later, another sound reached my straining ears.

My car starting up. Followed by the crunch of tires on gravel as it drove away.

Shivering sheep sherbet!

Gavin had taken my car. Worse than that, I knew precisely where he was headed. And who he was headed for.

I scrambled out of my hiding place and, flashlight beam bobbing all over the place thanks to my shaking hands, made it back to the clearing. From there, I ran along the path—more cardio, yay me—then up the driveway to hammer on Birdie's front door.

It wasn't Birdie who flung it open. Instead, I had the dubious pleasure of coming eyeball-to-eyeball with Cora, who appeared even less pleased to see me than if I'd been a charity collector asking for donations. "What do you wa—"

Bent double, the laptop clutched to my stomach, I wheezed, "Give me...the keys...to-your-car."

Note to self: download fitness app instead of playing Candy Crush.

"Where's your car? You were just driving it—hey!"

Having spied the fluffy pink pom-pom of her key chain

on Birdie's hall table, I'd made a desperate lunge for it. I snatched it up, but it slithered through my still-trembling fingers. Really wasn't in any shape to drive on dark country roads right now.

Before I could scoop up her keys again, Cora beat me to it and held them above her head like a schoolyard bully. "What is the matter with you? Are you having a seizure?"

What was it with me and mean girls? Did I attract them with some sort of invisible tattoo on my forehead that only they could see? I held up a finger and took three deep, wobbly breaths.

"I know who killed Alastair Brown, and he just tried to kill me." Okay, maybe a slight exaggeration. Gavin might've just wanted to indulge in a spot of late-night hide-and-seek. Perhaps, in this case, with some rather unpleasant consequences when the seeker found the hider. "And he stole my car after I mentioned that April was moving to Christchurch, and I found Dominic's laptop in a pile of kitty litter…"

Running out of oxygen, I stared helplessly into Cora's narrowed eyes.

"Do you need me to drive you to the emergency room?" she asked.

"No. Drive me to April's house because he's going after her. Please. He's already got a head start."

She stared at me a moment longer before lowering her arm. "Let's go."

Bless her heart, Cora Rossi drove toward town like a demon reincarnated as a rally driver, and we arrived outside April's place in a handbrake skid—or close enough. The car's headlights swept over the bumper of my car, parked in April's driveway.

Gavin was already here.

Not for the first time, I wasn't enjoying being right.

On the drive to April's, I'd left a garbled voicemail for Detective Mana and then contacted emergency services. Yes, priorities, I know. But I trusted the burly detective more than I did the system. Given that I sounded like the hysterical person I was, I hadn't made much headway in getting the operator to understand the situation.

I shoved my phone into Cora's hands, together with Marcus's laptop. "Keep this safe. I'm going in."

"No—what? You're insane. Wait for the police."

A tinny voice squawked out of my phone's speaker—probably telling me the same thing.

"When the cops get here, tell them Gavin Schmidt killed Alastair." I opened the door and jumped out. "I hope he hasn't hurt her already, and maybe he won't if there's a witness."

Cora made a growling sound as she twisted to retrieve something from the footwell of the back seat. "Take this with you then," she ordered.

My jaw went slack. "Seriously? You carry a baseball bat in your car?"

"Shut up and take it."

I took it.

"Go for the soft spots if he so much as looks at you sideways—eyes, throat, groin. Don't hesitate." She dismissed me with a glance and returned her attention to the operator.

Maybe we could be friends after all.

I hefted the bat and power walked down the driveway. Most of the lights were off in April's house, but her front door stood wide open. From inside came raised voices.

Gavin's gravelly and harsh with anger.

April's an octave higher than normal and nails-raked-down-a-chalkboard shrill.

Hairs puckering to attention on my nape, I felt both hot and clammy at the same time. If I'd been wearing the fitness tracker my sister gave me for Christmas, I suspect it would've exploded.

As I edged into the box-lined hallway, something smashed farther inside the house, the sound propelling me through another doorway and into April's kitchen. Harsh white light stabbed my eyeballs, momentarily dazzling me and casting a fuzzy glow around April, who wore a wonkily belted robe over her nightshirt. Gavin loomed over her, trapping her against the kitchen counter with his palms braced on either side. Spilled water and broken glass lay scattered around her bare feet. Guess I shouldn't expect much help from her should this situation escalate.

Taking advantage of the fact neither of them had spotted me yet, I put the bat down on a dining chair—its handle within easy reach. Back in the day, I'd been one of the last to be picked for ball sports. Although I had to admit, the team leaders had a justifiable reason for choosing the kid with their arm in a cast over me.

"Gavin," I shouted at his profile.

His head whipped around; his mouth slashed into a scowl. "You again?"

"Don't you hurt her," I said.

"Hurt her? I'm not going to hurt her—*I love her.*" His furious expression melting to puppy-dog pleading, he turned back to April. "I love you. You know that, right? After everything I've done for you."

April's knuckles whitened as her fingers clenched the counter edge. "You killed Alastair." Her words came out in a coarse whisper.

"Yeah, but I had to. I already explained everything. You said you understood."

"I do, but I—"

Gavin leaned in, and I took a sidestep closer to Cora's bat.

"Tell me I'm your hero," he demanded. "Tell me you love me and we can be together."

April seamed her lips closed and darted a glance in my direction. I couldn't risk saying anything that might set him off, so instead, I arranged my thumbs and index fingers into a heart shape and directed a play-along look at Gavin.

Slipping me a discreet blink of successful communication, she pried a hand away from the counter and squeezed Gavin's bicep. Adopting a suitably sappy expression, she said, "Thank you for rescuing me, and of course I love you, you big lug."

As the rigid tendons carving valleys in this neck softened, he turned his head to smirk at me. "See, I knew she did, deep down."

Deep, deep, deep down. So deep you'd need a backhoe to uncover it if April's current disgusted grimace was any indication.

Calling on my inner greeting-card composer, I pasted a smile on my lips. "True love wins out in the end."

I kept the smile in place while visually strip-searching the room, trying to figure out my next move. With any luck, the first responders would be here at any moment, but in the meantime, Gavin had two potential hostages in the house.

And while I suspected he meant what he said about not hurting April—at least if she played along with the true-love crap—the same couldn't be said for me...

THINK, Tessa. Think.

"April needs to change," I blurted.

"Change what?" Gavin's brow wrinkled. "She's perfect the way she is."

Oh my word, as Birdie would say. If this was what true love did to your gray matter, I wanted no part of it.

"She is," I said in the same tone I'd use with a not-very-bright customer who wanted to argue with me about whether the yarn color was blue or turquoise or azure. "But if you're taking off together tonight, she can't very well go in her nightie and robe, can she?"

He glanced down at April's attire as if only just noticing it. "Oh, yeah. Babe, you'd better go get dressed."

"And pack a bag," I added. "So you're ready to bug out with your boyfriend." I hoped she'd pick up on my silent 'get out of the house as fast as you can.'

Taking a step backward, Gavin crunched his heel down on a fragment of glass. "Oops. Watch your step." He lifted April over the broken shards.

She stared up at him, her upper lip curled. If he'd been looking at her face instead of the floor, it would have exposed the whole 'Bonnie and Clyde' lovebird act for what it really was. A big fat lie.

Don't screw this up and set him off, I ordered her with my stern gaze.

April modified her lip curl into a smile and squeezed his arm again. She stood close enough to the dining table now to spy the handle of Cora's baseball bat, and when she met my eyes, I knew she'd figured out my half-assed plan. "Gavin, darling, can you clean up the broken glass while I'm getting dressed? The dustpan and brush are in the pan—"

"Cabinet under the sink." I raised my voice over April's

and, at her frown, quickly added, "Bottom shelf, right at the back."

"Sure," he said with a smile. "Don't muck about. We've got to get out of here."

"Promise you won't even have time to miss me." April blew him a kiss and gave me a good-luck nod before disappearing into the hallway.

"You will take care of her, won't you?" I said in faux 'impressed you're such a gentleman' admiration.

"Always," he promised.

In his mind, he was, without a doubt, the hero of every chick flick he'd ever been forced to watch.

Gavin turned away from me and opened the cabinet. He knelt in front of it and ducked his head to rummage through whatever stuff April kept in there.

This was David's chance to fell Goliath; Harry Potter's opportunity to thwart Voldemort; Luke Skywalker's shot at the Death Star. Take your pick.

I took mine—Cora's baseball bat—and tip-toed toward Gavin's back. Within three heartbeats, I stood face-to-face with him. Well, face to him on hands and knees, butt stuck high in the air, head almost under the top shelf. Gripping the bat's handle, my palms felt greasy while the muscles in my arms possessed the same tensile strength as overcooked spaghetti.

Could I take a swing at him? Could I deliberately slam this potential weapon down on the white-and-hairy strip of exposed skin poking out of Gavin's jeans? What if I paralyzed him for life—could I live with that?

Stop dithering, Tessa! Do something!
So I did.

I used the bat as a big ol' poking stick and gave him one thumping prod in the rear.

Gavin collapsed forward with a yelp and sprawled flat on his belly.

Once again not waiting to check on the state of his tailbone, I dashed for the back door. With a wrench, I tore it open and all but fell through it...

Straight into a solid brick wall.

In fact, a brick wall would've felt like a goose down pillow compared to the unyielding chest of none other than Detective Sergeant Mana.

He wrapped an arm around my waist and held me against him as my legs gave way. With my eyes squeezed shut, I rested my face against the crisp cotton of his shirt, my arms anchoring themselves around his torso.

Safe. I was safe.

His deep voice vibrated against my cheek as he barked orders at unseen underlings. While chaos and an explosion of unidentifiable sounds erupted around and behind me as cops swarmed April's kitchen, I kept my eyes shut and made like a limpet clinging to a rock.

The rock being Eric. Because there's no way the detective sergeant would permit himself to hold a civilian like this nor stroke a big palm up and down her back. Eric Mana would, though, because despite wearing armor made of what appeared to be solid granite, beneath that hard exterior ran warmth and passion. Lava hot.

I could've clung to that rock face forever.

Unfortunately, there was no fade to black and rolling credits in this particular movie of my life. Reality sucks.

"Tessa." The cop had returned to his voice. With a sigh, I peeled my cheek off his chest and met his gaze. He didn't remove his arm from my waist, but his expression had become bland and unreadable. "This paramedic wants to check you over. Okay?"

"Okay." As I glanced sideways at the woman watching me with a mixture of concern and amusement, I realized I was still wrapped around Eric.

"Can you stand by yourself?" he asked.

Nope, so you'd better swoop me up into your arms *Officer and a Gentleman* style. "Yep. Sure thing."

Like gum stuck to a shoe sole, I eased myself away from Eric. Without meeting his gaze—because I was pretty sure he'd notice me looking at him as if I expected him to sprout wings and a halo—I shuffled over to the paramedic.

"I'll check in with you later, Ms. Wakefield," the detective said behind me.

And...dismissed.

"I know the drill," I muttered, allowing the woman to lead me over to a patio seat. Without acknowledging Eric's amused grunt, I sat before my wobbly legs gave out.

EIGHTEEN

The next morning, I decided to spend a few hours restocking Unraveled's shelves before news of my butt-poking shenanigans and Gavin's arrest hit the Cape Discovery grapevine. Actually, the tactile comfort of squishy yarns combined with the sounds of Kit and Pearl chasing a ping-pong ball around my feet was more of a self-soothing lifesaver.

Stifling a yawn, I reached for the hair-raising double-shot latte Rosie had dropped off a few minutes ago. Together with a selection of muffins and pastries, which spoke volumes of how worried she was about me. Of course, her fierce hug and 'you're such a walking disaster zone' had given her away first.

A few more sips of caffeine-infused ambrosia and I could fool my brain into believing I hadn't been up half the night dealing with the long arm of the law—and the more stressful interrogation from my family. The Spanish Inquisition had nothing on Harry and my mother. Good cop, bad cop? Try bad cop, worse cop.

Apparently, I was grounded for the next decade.

As for Sean, in his opinion, my bat-wielding skills made the best joke punchline ever. But he was also struggling to get his head around one of his mates being arrested for murder. Which meant that when he turned up on our doorstep on his way to a painting job, his usual ragging on me had been lackluster at best.

Pearl had just stolen the ping-pong ball and was heading for a goal shot under a shelf when a volley of knocks rattled the front door. It was a good fifteen minutes until the store officially opened, but that sounded like one impatient customer desperate for a merino or alpaca hit. Hopefully, they had really deep pockets to compensate for making me jump out of my skin.

I stepped out from behind the shelf and discovered it wasn't a yarn addict hammering on the door.

It was Oliver.

And he looked...well. Like a country song where his woman's left him for another cowboy, his last whiskey bottle's empty, and they've just repossessed his prize pickup truck. Mournful and mighty cheesed off at the same time.

I briefly contemplated bolting upstairs to hide under my trusty crocheted blanket but lost that option when both Kit and Pearl raced to the door and started yowling.

Attention seekers.

And a dead giveaway that I was somewhere close by.

Suck it up, sunshine, I told myself and crossed over to the front of the store. Totally expecting him to be clutching a damages bill—courtesy of the two felines standing on their hind legs and pawing at the glass. Or... actually, I couldn't come up with a second reason why Oliver might be irritated-and-heading-toward-hopping-mad with me.

I unlocked the door, but before I could fully open it,

Oliver barreled inside. The cats skittered off to hide under the armchairs.

"Are you...? You didn't—and I nearly—" As he broke off with a word Harry would've demanded a gold coin donation to his swear jar for, I backed up.

Wary but not afraid of the man in front of me, whose hair stood spiky and uncombed, flattened on one side of his head as if he'd just rolled out of bed.

Oliver pinched the bridge of his nose, then pointed a finger at me and scowled. "Mac called in sick this morning, 'and by the way, boss, did you hear about what happened on my street last night, involving that woman with all the cats?'" He blew out his cheeks. "I had no freaking clue what he was talking about."

"Oh." *That's* why he looked as mad as a mama wasp. "I've only got the two. Hardly enough to say 'all' the cats."

His eyebrows shot up. "That's what you're taking from this? Not that you could've been hurt—or worse—by a deranged killer? Or that you didn't call me?"

"Hey, I called the cops. That was my priority at the time."

"And getting all cozy with that city detective." The bitterness in his tone felt like biting on tinfoil, but it was the almost invisible thread of male jealousy woven through his accusation that made my cheeks heat and my stomach do a flippity-flop.

Well, two could play at that game. "Paramedic's one of your groupies, huh?"

His poker face firmly in place, Oliver turned and locked the store door before facing me again, arms folded over his broad chest. "Mac's sister-in-law. Quite the clinch she found you and the detective in."

"His name's Eric. And he's a detective *sergeant*." I

refused to surrender any more ground on this battlefield. If he wanted to come out and ask me if something was going on between Eric and me, he could fire the first shot.

"I know his name. And his rank," Oliver snapped. "What I don't know is why I had to find out what happened from one of my staff. I thought we were friends."

"Is that what we are? Friends?" I'd planned on the word coming out dripping with snark, but instead, it slid off my tongue in a lamb's bleat. Once I'd cleared the frog in my throat, I tried again: *"Friends* don't publicly announce that they'll ask another friend on a date and then not get around to it for weeks. *Friends* don't make another friend think they're finally going on a date when, in reality, they're visiting a nursing home. If we're *just* friends, stop sending me mixed signals."

So much for not firing the first shot.

At the creasing of his forehead, I threw my hands in the air and stalked away from him—intending to, I dunno, get all stabby with a pair of nine-millimeter steel knitting needles. However, I'd taken no more than three stomping steps before Oliver grabbed my arm and spun me around. Twice within the space of twelve hours, I found myself mushed up against a handsome man's chest.

Two *different* handsome men. A new record.

Through the warm cotton of Oliver's T-shirt, my fingertips detected the rapid thumping of his heartbeat. Mine accelerated to match it in a drag race when his big work-roughened palm cupped my jaw and tilted my chin to the right angle.

The right *kissing* angle.

Which he then proceeded to do in a most un-friend-like fashion, forcing me to backpedal until my butt hit the shelf behind me.

Balls of yarn bounced off my head; I scarcely registered it.

Claws skittered on the floor as my cats pounced on the contraband; I couldn't have cared less.

The entire store could've fallen down around me, and I wouldn't have minded, as long as Oliver's lips didn't leave mine.

However, all too soon, they did. And with only a stroke of his knuckles across my cheek, he was gone.

Back to the grindstone, then.

Ten minutes after I'd opened the store, Harry fussing at my side behind the service counter, my phone buzzed with a text.

OLIVER: That shouldn't have happened. I'm sorry. You deserve a better man.

"BETTER THAN OLLIE?" Harry said beside me. "You'd be hard-pressed to find one."

My glance shot sideways to where my granddad was making no effort to hide his gawking at my phone. "Really, Harry? You're on his side?"

Harry chuckled. "There is no side. He's a good man; you're a good woman. And from the looks of it, I suspect he's a good kisser."

"You saw that?" I squeaked.

"Hard for even an old fella like me to miss when he comes into work to find his granddaughter lip-locked with the local bar owner and stock all over the floor."

"Sheesh." My face went nuclear. "Well, don't worry. It won't happen again. You read his text."

"Pah." Harry patted my shoulder. "Man doesn't kiss someone like that by accident, and he sure as eggs won't be able to stop himself at just one. You're like a gingernut biscuit, girlie. Totally addictive."

"Thanks. I think." I found a *don't care either way* smile for him and stuffed my phone back in my pocket. "Now, how about a nice cup of tea?"

"Ooh, yes, please. And some gingernuts to dunk in it."

At least it was easy to divert Harry's mind from kisses to snacks. I doubted I'd find it quite so easy to forget, though I planned to do my darnedest to try.

THINGS SOON SETTLED back to normal in my little corner of the world. At least, as normal as it gets within the whirlwind circle of my nutty family. Harry fussed over me for a day before returning to his 'tough love—you're okay' brand of affection. Dad fussed by bringing me a couple of potted plants, which he promised to keep an eye on because of my botanic homicidal tendencies. My siblings fussed by bombarding me with iMessages and sometimes inappropriate funny GIFs. And Mum, well, Mum just fussed.

As for my friends...

My Wednesday evening get-together with Rosie came as a welcome respite. Leaving her husband to supervise the bath and bedtime routine, Rosie and I retired to her formal dining room and locked the door behind us. To play Scrabble. You heard me, Scrabble. Cocktail's worth fifty-four points if you hit a triple word score. Whilst dissecting the week's events, lamenting our parent/sibling/spouse/grandfather irritations, and solving world peace, Rosie and I are rather partial to a Cuba libre. Or two.

Birdie's informally adopted Cora as her granddaughter after the DNA test revealed she was undeniably related to Samuel MacKenzie. She'd dragged Cora along to last Tuesday's beginners class and had looked as proud as a mama bear when her prodigy completed a magazine-perfect sample of knitted rows. Turns out Cora isn't a sea urchin. More one of those fake cacti decorations that look vicious and mean, but the prickles are bendy rubber when you apply a little pressure. We both looked after Birdie during Dominic's funeral, and somehow, during the refreshment part of it, I found myself offering to organize Cora's baby shower.

I have no idea how that happened. She mentioned pink and blue frosted cupcakes, and my mouth ran away with me.

And I haven't as yet decided whether Oliver and/or Eric Mana fitted neatly into the 'friends' column.

I'd managed to avoid accompanying Harry to Friday night happy hour at the Stone's Throw for the past two weeks. Although it had required a degree of bribery and corruption to rope Sean into playing wingman to our granddad on a guys' night out, it was worth every cent of the tab I'd set up with Lucinda to avoid running into Oliver and his kissable lips again. At least until I figured out what column he belonged in.

But moving on to other, more pleasant, dilemmas.

Dilemmas such as what to take to our first Crafting for Calmness potluck dinner, being hosted by Beth Chadwick at six p.m. sharp. The Serial Knitters and Happy Hookers had called a temporary truce and bonded over the idea of Beth's secret-recipe fried chicken and George's Mars Bar cheesecake. All I had to do was figure out what to bring, so I found myself at the Sunday morning farmers market in search of inspiration.

Marcus Hall's produce stall was conspicuous by its absence. Little wonder, as they'd arrested him the day after Gavin—who'd presumably sung like the proverbial canary.

Having selected some green beans and a cauliflower, I was examining a squash when I became aware of a presence next to me. A giggling presence dressed in denim dungarees, gumboots, and sparkly fairy wings. They go with everything, don't you know?

"Vicky." I braced my stomach muscles in anticipation of her uncle popping up from behind a stand of butternut pumpkins. "You're looking magical this morning. Cast any spells on your Uncle Eric lately?"

"Nope." Her gaze darted to a spot behind me, forewarning me of Uncle Eric's imminent arrival. "But I could turn Uncle Ricky into a toad, and then you could kiss him and turn him into a handsome Prince Charming." She made kissy-kissy sounds and chortled.

Probably at the pained expression I saw on her uncle's face when I turned around. His expression aside, the sight of him caused a significant rise in my blood pressure. Dressed in what appeared to be his standard off-duty autumn attire of jeans and a sweater—another fisherman's rib, this one in navy blue—this time, he wasn't alone. Elbow linked through Eric's, a stunning black-haired woman stood at his side, also dressed in a sweater and jeans—the skinny kind that highlighted her catwalk-model figure.

I nodded a greeting, the muscles in my jaw aching with the effort of not laughing along with the little girl, and then from the irrationally jealous frown my mouth wanted to assume. "Hello, Eric." I nipped the edge of my tongue to halt the automatic 'how are you?' or 'nice to see you' social pleasantry that wanted to roll off it afterward.

If you're familiar with Miss Manners' advice on making small talk with a tall, dark, and brutally handsome cop that one's kinda developing a crush on, please do get in touch.

"Hello, Tessa," he said, just as formally in return.

"You're *Tessa*?" Next to him, the woman's full lips parted to reveal a toothy smile, and before she'd even slid her arm out of Eric's, I recognized it. "I've heard so much about you."

"And you must be Vicky and Simon's mum." I enjoyed the panicked flare in Eric's eyes as they shifted to his sister-in-law.

Perhaps he was imagining the multitude of sinful things she could reveal about him.

She stepped in front of Eric and embraced me, kissing me on the cheek as though we were the best of friends instead of complete strangers. "*Kia ora*, Tessa. I'm Mari."

While this might appear strange to an outsider, it was the everyday warmth of Māori culture on display, and I grinned at her. "Your kids are gorgeous."

"Must take after their dad." Mari gave me a wink. "And their Uncle Ricky."

Uncle Ricky muttered something unintelligible under his breath and glared at a pyramid of stacked pumpkins instead of meeting my eyes. I almost expected the heat of his stare to trigger some latent telekinesis and send the vegetables tumbling.

"Hardly toad-like at all." Mari elbowed him in the ribs.

I decided to put him out of his misery. "Can you tell me anything about Gavin and Marcus?" I asked. "Will I have to testify at their trials?"

Eric cleared his throat, relief evident in every line of his big body at the security of talking about work as opposed to more personal topics. "Undecided. Both men made full confessions but haven't entered formal pleas yet. However, I'm confident that they'll plead guilty and save everyone the hassle of going forward."

"I hope so. How about Dominic's laptop?"

He grimaced. "The techs are having a field day with it. There are a few men and women around who are poorer but now much wiser since being contacted."

"Ouch. Love hurts," I said.

"Or exists only in fairytales if you believe him." Mari tipped her head toward Eric.

Vicky skipped over to us and wrapped her arms around her mother's legs. "I love fairytales. Last night, Uncle Ricky read me the one where the princess kisses the toad. He told me I'd have to kiss a lot of toads before I found a nice boy." Her nose crinkled. "But I don't wanna kiss toads...or boys. Boys are gross and smelly. Except for Daddy and Uncle Ricky. I'm going to marry Uncle Ricky when I grow up." She sent me a challenged-filled stare. "So you'd better not kiss him after all."

Eric made a choking sound and clapped his palm over his eyes. Ah, kids. They say the darnedest things.

"I promise I won't steal your future Prince Charming," I told Vicky in the most serious tone I could muster.

Mari stroked her daughter's head, her amused gaze meeting mine.

"Pinky swear?"

"Pinky swear." I offered Vicky my bent finger.

Once we'd sealed the deal to her satisfaction, Vicky turned and grabbed Eric's hand to pull him forward a couple of steps. "Can we go get some hot chips now? You promised."

"I did." He sent me an apologetic but relieved glance.

A dull red flush continued to spread across his cheekbones, making it necessary for me to slot him into a newly created column in my mental spreadsheet, titled: Men I like but with Whom I have No Foreseeable Future. I felt my own face grow warmer than the weak autumn sunshine justified.

"We must meet up for coffee and a chat sometime," Mari said as her daughter snatched up her other hand. "I can see we have something in common."

Like an attraction to tall, dark, and handsome men? Unattainable and inappropriate in my case.

But under the unreadable stare of Detective Sergeant Mana, I adopted a confident, slightly knowing smile. Letting him remain uncomfortable at the idea of his sister-in-law sharing secrets with the annoying woman who kept stumbling into his ordered world, I said, "It's a date."

ABOUT THE AUTHOR

Tracey Drew lives Down Under with her husband—who's given up complaining about her yarn addiction—and two madcap tabby cats called Kevin and Alfie. The feline brothers constantly battle with her while she's trying to write her books by demanding lap-time, but they also provide constant inspiration for her fun & quirky cozy mysteries.

Printed in Great Britain
by Amazon